A Gift From Daddy

Frank Hutchison

MR PUBLISHING

Published by
MR Publishing, LLC
Roswell, GA 30075

ISBN: 978-0-9797482-4-0

Printed in the United States of America
Original cover design by Fran Conn

To Mister:

You are the best bub in the whole world, and no matter what happens, always remember that daddy loves you whole bunches.

A Gift From Daddy

1 RAIN BEGAN FALLING IN THE LATE AFTERNOON, AND thunder pounded through the sky seemingly harder than ever before. The drops smacked against the windshield as the car approached its destination.

The quiet serenity of his car masked the pain that Tom felt at that moment for he had spent the majority of the day making arrangements for his dad. His face was stern, his clothes wrinkled and quickly thrown together, but for a change, there was no hurry. He had been driving now for two hours trying to overcome his feelings of loss and pain, but so far, all he had become was numb—the kind of numb you get when all you have is running on empty and you think that all hope is gone.

"Why?" he cried aloud.

"Why now? Why do this now? I still need you in my life. I need your guidance. Damn you for leaving!" he screamed, as the tears streamed down his face and he pounded the steering wheel.

He had been struggling with the same question for a long while, and the answers were not coming. The numbness actually worked to separate his thoughts from his emotions, but the dull ache in his belly would not go away. Somehow, he sensed that his car understood his need to be alone, and respectfully, it was running more quietly than it had in a couple of years.

What would Dad think of me right now if he saw his son with tears in his eyes? He thought to himself.

A slight grin appeared on his face as he thought of what his dad's words would be... *Are you kidding me with this? You are a grown man for Christ's sake. Get a grip.*

His father always had an in-your-face attitude about life, which was one of the many things Tom loved most about him. Tom Sr. was an ex-Marine whose life can be told in two parts. After he left the Marines, he worked as an installation technician for the local phone company. It was a good living, but he never felt truly fulfilled. Then at age thirty-six, he changed his life completely. He started taking night classes at the local college, and within five years, he had obtained his bachelor's degree. Soon after, he decided to start investing in real estate, and by the time he turned forty-seven, he was retired. He never let anybody forget about his military background, and many people believed that it was his Marine training that made him so successful in business.

Physically, he was a strong man, standing six feet tall and made of pure muscle. His frame was stout, proportioned, and best described as stocky. More than anything else, one glance told people that Tom Sr. was not a man to be taken lightly. He had a hard edge that most people wouldn't mess with, and he used its power well.

Throughout the neighborhood, it was known that Tom Sr. didn't play by anybody's rules but his own. Fortunately, he was a fair man who demanded and commanded respect from not only his own son, but also all the other kids as well. Away from the public, he had a softer side and a deep love and affection for his family which showed itself more and more in his later years. He was, by definition, a complex yet intriguing puzzle to all but a select few who knew him well.

The high, black iron gates adorned the entrance to the long and curvy driveway of the main building. Tom slowly turned his car into the road, ready to take the journey he never wanted to take. His stomach began to ache more definitively, and his first impulse was to turn the car around and drive away. He also knew that he had no choice but to continue.

As he pulled his car into the lot, he took a quick glance out the window and noticed a haunting reality. The grave marking flowers were aligned symmetrically on their marks, forming what looked like dots of a connecting puzzle standing at attention—either paying homage to those who had gone before or acting as sirens for those to come. Tom sat in his car, his hands still on the wheel, trying to make his aching body move. The pain came and went, and all he could think about was how all of this had come at the wrong time.

My life has gone to hell in the past thirty-six hours, he thought to himself. How can everything be fine and then suddenly change? *How can you, one minute, have today and tomorrow and, the next, have only a memory?*

"Damn you, Dad!" he yelled. "Damn you!"

Glancing around the parking lot, he noticed that his wife, Sara, and son, Tommy, must already be inside since her car was parked across the way. Fortunately, Sara understood that Tom needed his space today and had let him do what he needed to cope. This understanding is just one example of how well Sara knew Tom and why he considered her the love of his life.

As he opened the car door and stepped out onto the pavement, he saw the sign directly in front of him—BEDFORD MEMORIAL GARDENS—a place he would have wished to never see again. The building was ornate in appearance and looked more like a golf course clubhouse than it did a funeral home. The outside was white stone, like the columns in the entrance, and the starkness of the color apparently was supposed to bring cheer to those who entered. The steps were long and narrow to the door, and Tom took them slowly. His mind flashed back to when he was three years old, and his dad was holding his hands as he stuck out his foot and awkwardly tried to climb the stairs in his home. He remembered how scared he was then and how determined he was to show his dad that he was big. He knew his dad's presence and support provided him warmth and comfort, and his dad was a source of strength throughout his thirty-five years. Although there were times he turned away to find his own footing, he always knew his dad was there. This was another example of how his mind had raced all day remembering images, smells, and memories of things he had either forgotten or didn't think he knew.

At the top of the stairs, he encountered John Bedford, funeral director and owner. John was a unique fellow with a receding hairline and a large, dumpy frame. John had been in the funeral business for more than thirty years, and he had presided over the funerals of all four of Tom's grandparents. Although a strange man, John was a 'take charge' spirit and a kind soul, an important comfort in his line of work.

"Tom, if you need anything at all, just let me know," he said. "Just follow the corridor until you reach the small staircase on the left. You will see the room from there."

"Thanks John," Tom replied quietly. "You've been a tremendous help to my family and me, and I do appreciate it."

John smiled warmly back at Tom and his warmth made him feel better for the moment. A couple of deep breaths later, Tom was at the top of the stairs. For the first time since the call from his mother, he was about to face his reality—the death of his father. Not that he hadn't felt it all day making arrangements, but this time, he would actually see his dad lying there still and lifeless.

The sign in the doorway read—THOMAS PHILLIPS, SR—and a cold chill ran through Tom's body. "Damn you for not saying goodbye," he said silently as he passed by the sign and headed into the room. Quickly, he gathered himself to meet and greet those who came to pay their respects. The idea of keeping a smile on and being friendly didn't exactly appeal to him at the moment, but Tom knew that at the very least, this would be a convenient time to see friends and family he only saw during holidays, weddings, and funerals.

Look at my family. It's funny how families are created and develop as years go by. You would think that instead of pushing each other away and becoming estranged that we would want to remain close and involved, but the opposite is usually true. In the end, all we have is our family, yet the way we behave, how could you ever know who was family and who was not?

Tom encountered his Aunt Cindy and they stopped and talked for a while. Cindy was his father's youngest sister. She and Tom Sr. were two years apart in age, and he was her protector. They were very close. She always treated Tom like her own son, since she had two girls. She would always tell him that he was the son she never had, and she made sure he felt special. That always worked well for him as a child because he could count on Aunt Cindy to buy him things his parents would not.

"Are you holding up okay?" Tom asked with a forced grin.

"I'm doing okay. Getting through the initial shock is the hardest part," she added. "Now, I'm starting to remember the good times. How are you doing?"

"I'm fine," Tom responded, lying for the first of many times to come that evening. "Have you seen Sara and Tommy?" At that time, he saw his wife enter the room. His son, Tommy, was right by her side looking a little frightened and confused. Tom excused himself and went to them.

"Hey stranger. How are you holding up? We were worried a bit about you today," Sara said with a warm smile.

"I'm doing a lot better, considering," Tom replied, knowing that she could see right through him.

"Hey, son, are you doing okay?" Tom asked.

"I'm fine," Tommy replied. Then, as if knowing it was what his father needed most, Tommy reached over and gave his dad the biggest hug a ten-year-old could muster. The feeling of strength and love coming from his son was almost too overwhelming for Tom, but he didn't let go.

"Daddy, I love you whole bunches," Tommy said. It was a phrase that Tom Sr. used to say to Tom when he was growing up, and since Tom always loved hearing his father say it, he decided he would use it with Tommy. Although Tommy didn't say it too much as he got older, he seemed to know that his dad would appreciate the kind thought.

"I love you whole bunches, too," Tom replied.

For the past couple of years, Tom and Tommy had grown a little apart, and signs of affection from his son were becoming more and more rare. Sara kept telling Tom that since Tommy was so much like him, it was hard for him to clearly see the things that frustrated them both. Although he believed her, Tom also believed that things would pass and that by staying active in his son's life and activities, Tommy would know his dad was there for him, that he was loved, and that he would eventually come around.

Tom had mentioned to Sara, and anyone who would listen over the years, his father's philosophy on children, and she was starting to believe it more and more as Tommy grew older. Tom Sr. called his philosophy the 'Adolescent Trilogy,' and he believed that parents could separate a child's life into three distinct stages as it related to their relationship with them. The three stages cover roughly the first twenty years or so of a child's life. Ranging from emotional and instructional to financial, the lessons Tom and Sara were learning seemed to be right on target with what Tom Sr. had been telling everyone all along.

Noticing that Tom was drifting, Sara looked up, "Me and Tommy are going to check on Cindy. We haven't seen her in a couple months."

Tom saw her flash her cute half-grin that he adored so much. *I'm so lucky,* he thought. *She knows I'm hurting and struggling; yet, she doesn't push to ask questions to which she already knows the answers.*

"Okay, I'll find you in a few minutes," Tom answered.

Looking across the room, Tom saw his mother, and their eyes met. He saw the redness in her eyes from the long hours of hurt she had been enduring. He could also feel the love from her eyes as she looked back at him, knowing his pain as well. His mother sat in a single chair near the casket so that friends and relatives could stop by after spending a moment paying respects to Tom Sr.

As Tom walked closer, he noticed that the walls, like the entrance, were painted stark white; and the carpet, a rich crimson. Flowers, piled seemingly to the ceiling, were strategically placed around the room. Tom's mind drifted for a moment as he took in his surroundings. *The irony was priceless,* he thought. *How could a room that breathed so much life be home to so much death? What could a room like this hope to accomplish?* Then Tom caught himself before sinking too deep.

"Damn," he said.

"TJ," his mother said as he got closer, her voice saying, *I'm here for you.*

Tom didn't like being called by his childhood name as he had grown older, but for some friends and family, he understood that the habit was hard to break. Sometimes, he would get frustrated with them because he felt they didn't try hard enough to break the habit, but ultimately, he tried to let it go.

"Yes," he answered. This time, however, he didn't grow frustrated or angry with her as it comforted him for a moment to be a child again.

"Come over here and give me a hug. I was looking for you earlier but couldn't find you. Are you alright?" she said as she outstretched her arms.

Tom hugged his mother and thought about what an amazing woman she is. She had lost her husband of thirty-six years; yet, she was consoling him. Circumstance changes nothing to a mother when her child is in need. Tom remembered how his father taught him the value of people. Character, he would say, shows itself when things are tough. Those are the times when people can be measured. As if he had any doubt, Tom knew his mother passed the test and then some.

"Yes, I'm fine," Tom lied again. "I just needed some time to get my head on straight. Sorry I wasn't here for you."

"Don't be silly. It's quite alright," she replied warmly. "I expected that you would."

As Tom took his place by his mother's side, he felt a presence he could not explain. The feeling was so strong, he actually had to look back to see if his father was still there.

Yes, I'm here, my son. Look at you both—my family—oh, how I miss you! I wish I could be there to comfort you right now, but it's not to be.

His mother grabbed him by the hand, so they could strengthen each other, and then turned to face the casket. She had avoided looking at Tom Sr. to both keep her composure and to wait for her son to be with her.

"Look at your Father. What a strong, proud man even in death," she said earnestly.

As they looked down on Tom Sr. in the open casket, dressed handsomely in his navy blue suit, it was obvious that she was right. In life, he was a strong man who was proud of himself, his family, and his son. Tom wanted so desperately to reach out, shake his father and wake him up. His mind was heavy with loss and despair, and he just wanted to have a few more minutes to say goodbye and to ask a couple more questions—seeking the advice he had come to know and trust.

What do I do next? How do I make it okay, now that it's my job to do? Tom thought. *Damn him.*

Tom found a chair and took a seat beside his mother near the end of the casket. Family and friends came and went, and Tom was amazed at how strong she was through it all. As for him, his strength came by casually making eye contact with Sara as she spoke with friends and family and by watching Tommy work his charm on his relatives.

"TJ." Tom knew the voice before he saw the face. It was Earl Johnson, or Uncle Earl, his dad's best friend.

"Yes," Tom answered, as he stood up to greet him.

"TJ, or should I say Dr. Phillips? I'm so sorry about this," Earl said, holding back his own tears. "I'm at a place where I just don't know what to do."

"Earl, thank you," Tom said warmly. "I don't think any of this has set in just yet for any of us."

"You know, your dad and I were supposed to go fishing this weekend. You know how he loved to be out on the water and fish all day."

"Yes, I do. What were you fishing for this weekend?" Tom asked.

"Well, we heard about how the stripe were supposed to be jumping in a creek off Lake Somerset. Your father and I hadn't been to that part of the lake yet, but you can imagine it from there. By dusk, we would be back at, or near, our regular spot fishing for perch," Earl said, shaking his head and grinning in a long moment of reflection. "I never could figure out why he liked fishing for them so much."

Earl continued, "Oh well, I'm going to speak with your mother for a while. You need anything, just let me know."

Tom and Earl hugged as men do with other men they care about. The embrace was solid and meaningful yet full of compassion and strength. Tom looked back at his father lying still in the casket. A lone tear made its way down his cheek as he was hit with the cold realization that he would never again hug his father like that. He felt the pain and fear race through his body, and his knees almost buckled before he gathered himself.

"Damn," he mumbled softly.

Later, as he lay awake in his bed, Tom couldn't help but think about his dad in the casket—so lifeless, so empty. Just a few days earlier, he had phoned his dad to plan one of their two yearly fishing trips. Tom had marked it down in his calendar and had arranged time off from work. The plan was to go the beginning of September.

Tom Sr. was talking about the thrill of catching large-mouth bass with a new top-water lure he had purchased and how patience was the key. He loved the competition of it all more than anything else, he would say. As for Tom, he was thinking while his dad spoke that it was going to be thrilling just to spend time with him.

Tom couldn't sleep, and he knew that Sara had a long day as well, so he made his way downstairs to his study. After sitting in his leather, high-back chair for nearly an hour in the dark, the tears began to flow, and his soul let go.

"Why? Why? Why?" he cried, as he slammed his hands hard on his desk. "Aren't we supposed to have all kinds of time with our parents? When they get into their golden years, aren't we supposed to be able to come together and be a part of their fruitful, long lives? Where does it say that some people will have this luxury and others won't? I still have things to learn from you, Dad. I still need your wisdom. I'm not ready for this."

When the last tear dried, the darkness called to Tom, and his spirit was empty. He was so in tune with his body that he could hear his blood pulsing...THUMP. THUMP. THUMP.

How I wish that I could help you, my son. I, too, thought that I had so much more time on this earth. I thought that I would be able to watch you grow old and become a grandfather yourself. But my life was to end and God had a different plan for me. I keep holding them off because I can't leave with you like this, or my soul will never sleep. You curse me, but I know you don't mean it. TJ, it's okay. How can I make you understand?

Tom jumped as he awoke in his chair. He quickly looked over at the fuzzy lit numbers, showing six o'clock in the morning. He had only been asleep for two hours, but he knew he would not be able to go back to sleep on this day. Tom had succumbed to the darkness as never before. During the night, he began to remember things about his dad—time spent, vacations, holidays—but the memories only gave way to tears of loss.

Initially, Tom wasn't a sensitive man. He had learned the art of emotional separation when his feelings began to stir; however, since he had met Sara and especially when Tommy was born, he began to feel things more deeply. Sara said it was a sign of maturity and the beginning of a new journey. Tom Sr. jokingly said he was getting in touch with his feminine side and that he wanted an explanation.

But in the early morning hours on the day he was to bury his father, Thomas Phillips Jr. cried like a baby. He cried for the times he and his dad disagreed; he cried for the strength his dad gave him; and he cried because he could never again put his arms around him and tell him he loved him—never again. He cried so much that he had nothing left to get out.

At one point during the night, Sara got out of bed and came downstairs to check on Tom. She heard his sobs and wanted to go to him and give him comfort, but she understood his need to be alone—to work it out for himself and not feel embarrassed about his feelings. It was all she could do to stay away, so she sat on the stairs and cried for him.

As the new day began to rise, Sara and Tommy awoke and started downstairs for breakfast. The day was dreary, much like everyone's mood, and the clouds were overcast and created an unusually cold wind for that time of year.

Tom made his way into the kitchen and sat down with his family. Tommy and Sara began to talk about different things to pass the time, but to Tom, the words were just sounds and nothing more. Tommy had never seen his dad like this before, and he was very hesitant to speak with him. Tom's eyes and face were still puffy from the night's events, and he hoped, for appearance's sake that a hot shower would bring him back around.

Sara mentioned that she and Tommy were going to run an errand before heading over to the service, and she reminded Tom that he was supposed to pick up his mother and bring her.

"Tom," Sara said.

"Yes."

"Did you hear what I said? Don't forget to pick up your mother."

"I won't."

Sara looked at him skeptically because he showed no emotion as he spoke. She had brought up the idea at the funeral home recognizing that the two of them would need that special time together before saying goodbye. As for Tom and his mother, they had no idea why Sara had suggested it, but they didn't mind at all.

Tom spent the rest of the morning going through his normal routine of getting ready, but the routine ended up taking him three hours because his mind kept drifting to other things. The funeral was set to start at three-thirty, so he left to pick up his mother at noon. During the ride, Tom barely spoke, and his mother was unusually quiet as well.

"TJ," she asked.

"Yes."

"Last night something strange happened to me. I was at home going through photo albums of my wedding and our family vacations, and for a little while, I could swear I felt your father there with me. I didn't know if I should tell you about it or not, but I can't explain it. Do you think I'm crazy?" she questioned.

Tom's heart jumped as he drove because he, too, had experienced the same thing last night, and he was more afraid to bring it up than she was.

"No, Mom. I don't think you're crazy at all," answered Tom. "In fact, I've heard that feelings like that are normal considering the situation."

Tom knew that if he opened up and told his mother about his own experience the night before, he would have had to explain his anger and the fear of the future he was now facing. He couldn't risk telling her because he hadn't been able to work it out for himself yet. Maybe someday he would change his mind, but not right now, not today.

At the funeral home, people were arriving in droves to pay last respects. Both Tom and his mother were surprised at how many people showed up and how many had a warm and loving story to tell about Tom Sr. As he looked up, Tom saw more of his father's fishing buddies arrive. Mike, Jim, and Bob had driven a long way from the lake for the funeral. Tom was comforted by their presence, as they had been his adopted uncles for a long time.

Once the private viewing was over, the funeral began. Tom, Sara, and Tommy were seated beside Tom's mother in the front pew. Flowers were placed around the casket and the sanctuary and brought color to the otherwise dismal surroundings. Tom Sr. had always said that at his funeral, he wanted three things. First, he wanted to be buried with photos of him and his family during happy times, so Tom and his mother had put Christmas and vacation pictures in his casket at the private viewing.

Secondly, Tom Sr. wanted to pay homage to his Scottish roots, and he requested that bagpipes play an old Scottish praise song. He always believed that bagpipes added a certain dignity to a funeral. He had witnessed such during a military funeral a while back, and it had always stayed with him.

Finally, Tom Sr. wanted everyone to sing *Amazing Grace*, his favorite church hymn, at the end of the ceremony. He also requested that it be sung *a cappella* as he believed that God intended the song to be sung that way.

The funeral service was a little different than most because there was no sermon to be given. Although he was a spiritual man with devout faith, Tom Sr. didn't attend church on a regular basis. He always felt that funerals were a celebration of fond memories and love, not a captive audience to save sinners.

Knowing her husband's wishes, Tom's mother had asked close friends and relatives to tell a funny story about Tom Sr. and how much he meant to them. There were to be ten speakers in all, and Tom was to go last. His mother had asked him if he wanted to speak and gave him the opportunity to decline. He had thought a lot about it during his two-hour drive the day before and decided that he needed to do it for his dad—more importantly, for himself. As the bagpipes faded, Tom remained focused on a single spot on the pew directly in front of him. He hadn't really had time to think about anything to say, and he honestly didn't know if he was going to be able to do it.

Ah, I love that song. So many nice things said about me today, and I realize how lucky I was. I see TJ staring intently at the pew, so he must still be worried about things. Maybe I just need to hear him send me off in his own way, and then it will be fine. I wish I could reach out to him and give him what he needs, but I just don't know how.

After Cindy sat down, Tom instinctively walked up to the podium to say his peace. The weight began to climb back on his shoulders, and he felt the burden all over again.

"I was asked by mom to eulogize my dad and his life," he began. "But when I think of how much he meant to me…" his voice trailed off. He stepped back from the podium, and the tears began to stream down his face. After a moment of grinding his teeth and locking his jaw to hold back further tears, Tom stepped up and began again.

"When I think of my dad, I think of a man who had a great and loving heart. I think of a man who would give his own life for mine. I think of a man who wasn't perfect, but whose spirit touched us all in one way or another," tearfully he said. "I just hope that I can be half the man he was, and I hope that I can somehow find the wisdom to know what to do going forward. I am a better man for knowing him."

Tom's words hung in the ears of everyone in attendance, and it was a few moments before they could gather themselves. As he sat down in his seat, both Sara and his mother grabbed a hand and squeezed it. As *Amazing Grace* began, there wasn't a dry eye in the sanctuary. Each bar was carefully examined and each word defined in detail. The service was over, and it was time to say goodbye.

At the gravesite, there was more of the same as friends and family began placing roses on the casket. Tom was particularly moved by Tommy as he approached the casket, bent over to kiss his grandfather for the last time, and deftly dropped his rose atop the pall. He then turned and stood by Tom with his arm around his waist—a place where he stayed until he, Tom, Sara, and Tom's mother arrived at the family home to greet guests and gather with friends and family bringing food. Tom mainly sat in a corner by himself, alternating his thoughts between hurt and anger. He still felt helpless and couldn't understand his emotions.

"Damn you for leaving," Tom mumbled again and again. "I'm thirty-five years old and I feel as lost as a child; yet, I'm responsible for everything now. Now, I'm supposed to be the leader—full of wisdom, whose sage words are to provide guidance to my family, to my mom, and more so, to my son. Yeah, right!"

So now I see more clearly what the issue is. How can I make you understand? How will we each ever have peace as I, too, carry this burden?

Sara and Tommy were listening to Earl describe one of many fishing trips that he and Tom Sr. had together. Tommy was listening intently and soaking up every word. Earl, aside from being a great friend to the family, was also one hell of a storyteller. When Tom was growing up, Earl used to tell him all kinds of stories. He later found out, half of which, weren't even true.

Tom looked up and caught Sara's eyes from across the room. The warmth from her eyes was so intoxicating that Tom longed to be alone with her—to cry on her shoulder and confront his fear with her.

"Dad," Tommy said.

"Dad," he said again slightly louder.

"Yes," Tom half answered.

"Dad, Grandpa and I were supposed to go fishing this summer, me and him alone for the first time," Tommy said sadly. "How will I ever learn to fish the right way?"

The clouds overtook Tom's vision as he listened to Tommy's words fade into the air. His body went numb, like it did the night before, and the darkness returned. He couldn't answer the question, and he sat there in a trance, his mind drifting away.

2

MY FATHER DIED A COUPLE OF MONTHS AGO, AND I can't seem to get it together. It's not like we were ever all that close, so it just doesn't make sense why I'm feeling this way.

Don't get me wrong, I loved him and he was a decent man, but we never really 'clicked' from the time I was twelve or so. Starting out, he was great. We would spend quality time together just playing and having fun, for I was a very active child. But as I grew older, it was like he didn't know what to do with me.

Sure, he did all the things that fathers do—take me to ballgames, coach my little league teams, and teach me to fish—but emotionally, he was shut down and guarded...never warm and inviting, always negative and upset with something or someone. My sister and I had a running joke where we would refer to him as 'the issue man.' We all have those people in our lives that always have an issue. God help them. What will they do to survive it all? Well, that was my father, so you can imagine how it was growing up in our house.

The strange thing is, though, that I miss the old bastard and his cantankerous ways. Sure, I shed some tears for him but not like I thought I would. I think I've just reached a point where I've come to terms with it; yet, I can't seem to get past my lack of interest in my work and my family. It's all strange to me—I don't really know why—but I'm hoping it will pass soon.

I've also decided that I've worked too long, doing the same things over and over, and I'm going to take a leave of absence for the spring and maybe the summer. Who knows? Maybe then I'll be back to normal and ready to go. I've heard of others taking time off, a sabbatical I think it's called, and when they returned, they were refreshed and had a clear mind. Besides, there's nothing like a good fishing trip to get the blood flowing again.

The original idea was to go and get away by myself for a while. Maybe not the whole summer but at least a few months. I thought that getting back to nature would be a nice change since growing up it was the only real place I could find peace. Jen, my wife, had other ideas.

I overheard her talking in the kitchen with TJ about the trip. Needless to say, he was not happy at all, but as I told Jen last night, he didn't have to go if he didn't want to—it would probably be more fun without him. Of course, I didn't say that part to her because I knew better, and I thought it best to leave it up to them.

"What do you mean you don't want to go?" Jen asked with a sharp tone and a piercing stare.

"Mom, it's my summer vacation, and it's nowhere near here. All my friends are going to be working summer jobs, hanging out at the pool, and having fun. Do you honestly believe that I would want to give up my entire summer to go fishing with Dad?" TJ said harshly.

"TJ, how dare you say something like that about your father," Jen answered quickly. "You know it would kill him to hear you say that."

"Would it?" TJ fired back.

"Now you listen to me and you listen good," Jen said sharply. "I realize that you are fifteen years old and you think you know everything, but you don't. As long as you live under my roof, you will do as I say, and unfortunately for you, you have no other options. You are going on this trip with your father, and that's final. I've gotten the school to allow you to take two exams early, and you can leave in two weeks without any problems."

"But Mom," TJ whined, knowing he had no chance.

"But nothing," Jen said firmly. "I'm tired of you both and your attitudes toward each other. You have the rest of your life to get over it, but you will do this for me."

After several moments of silence, I come into the room to find them both with tired looks on their faces. I decide to make light of the situation and pretend that I didn't hear anything. I figure it won't do any good since I know how TJ feels about me anyway, but what the hell.

"Tom," Jen said. "I was just speaking with TJ about your trip, and he said he wants to go with you." Of course, being married to her for sixteen years, I know she isn't being completely truthful. Even if I hadn't overheard her a few moments ago, I know her poker face.

"Is that right? Well then, we'll have a great time, and I look forward to it. How about you, Son, doesn't it sound exciting to you too?"

"Yeah, Dad. It'll be great," TJ said as he stands up and storms off to his room.

I see the look he gives Jen as he leaves, and he's not happy. I think he feels his own mother is betraying him, and he can't do anything about it. I look back at Jen, and I feel the hurt she is trying to hide. I know I should do something, but I really don't know what to do. So, as the case has been lately, I do nothing.

Recently, I've discovered that's the way it is in our family. We have a great way of making the people we care about most feel hurt and upset. My guess is that this happens in all families, and it seems like we have it down to a science. We talk to each other harshly. We act like we don't care, and sometimes, I question if we really don't. I don't like what I've uncovered.

Just like right there—we all are feeling things; yet, we sugar coat what we say, or we don't say it at all. I'm not critical of them—because I'm probably the worst of the bunch—but that's how it is among us. We just don't communicate anymore.

Sure, Jen and I get along fine, but I can't reach TJ. His head is always somewhere else. He doesn't listen or care. It's like the aliens have come down and taken him away, and they've replaced him with someone who looks like my son but doesn't act like him.

Over the next two weeks, I take care of finalizing the arrangements and getting ready for the trip, while TJ finishes up his exams and his freshman year. I can't believe how good it feels to be going somewhere. Maybe it's that I get to go fishing—something I truly love—or maybe it's just time away from the daily grind of work. I don't know, but I like the thought of it a lot.

TJ has been in a foul mood for these past couple of weeks and has barely spoken to me at all. That's not really all that different from what normally happens between us. But he also hasn't spoken to his mother that much, and that is unusual.

On the Tuesday before we leave, I figure I would try to bury the hatchet and make the best of the situation. So I sit down with TJ at the table, and I try to show him where we're going and why I think it'll be a great place to go. He doesn't care. He asks no questions and barely acknowledges my existence. I know right then and there that we're going to be in for a long trip.

I know he's not happy, and I really can't blame him for that. Jen is insisting that we go, and I'm not going to go back on my word to her. After all, I realize that I haven't been that pleasant to be around lately either, and I think she needs the break as much as I do.

So I guess now I'm stuck with TJ and his attitude for the duration of the trip. My hope is that he'll either lighten up or leave me alone because this trip is for me to take some time, try to relax, and to work some things out—things that were never resolved.

Saturday morning arrives, and we're ready to go. Jen makes some sandwiches for the trip and has them wrapped on two separate plates. TJ is moving as slow as he possibly can to make sure that we both know how mistreated he is and how bad he has it. I lean into Jen to give her a kiss goodbye. Instead, she wraps both her arms around me and gives me a tight, meaningful hug, and I feel the love that she has for me.

"I'm going to miss you so much," she said.

"I know, and I'm going to miss you too. I'll be back before you know it. The trip should take about eight hours, and I'll call you once we get there to let you know which cabin we'll be staying in."

TJ gives his mother a half hug, and I see the expression on his face that says, *Oh boy, here we go.* Being the instigating soul that I am, I give the horn a quick press to move him along. Startled, TJ gives me a look that burns my soul. Oh yes, this is going to be a fun trip.

After the last clear radio station fades, I sit back and take in the scenery. I've decided to take back roads instead of the Interstate because I remember how much I enjoyed mountains and lakes as a kid. Let's face it, there's generally not a lot of scenery from the Interstate. Besides, I miss it. The only time I see trees and lakes, now, is when I go fishing, and that's not nearly often enough.

"So, where exactly are we going?" TJ asked, half interested.

"We're heading up to a great fishing place that Earl told me about last year. From what I understand, it's a grand lake stocked full of fish, and we will be staying in a little town named Ashwell."

"What made you decide to go there and spend the summer? It's not like you to go that far from home, much less for a whole summer," TJ asked showing his displeasure.

"Well, from what Earl told me, Ashwell is a small, quaint little town that looks like an old fishing village from way back, and it's a great place to catch many different types of fish. Most of the people who live there now have lived there all their lives. He also told me that the area is most famous for its yellow perch, which is the best tasting fish you can find, according to those who've eaten it."

"Okay," TJ mumbled.

"Really, I just thought it would be something different to do—something unlike me. Mostly, I plan on learning the area and spending the days fishing in the channels and the side creeks. If we don't catch anything, that'll be just fine. I just want to be out on the water and try to escape for a while. Either way, I think it'll be good. What do you think?"

"I don't know," TJ answered dryly.

"I reserved us a cabin on the lake so we can get early starts. Remind me to call your mother when we get there and let her know the unit number."

"Sure," TJ replied as he shifts his body in his seat trying to get comfortable. He obviously doesn't want to talk anymore as the front of his body is now facing the opposite direction.

I remember being his age and being with my father. I thought he was the stupidest man to ever live, and if I had a dime for every time he got under my skin, I would be rich.

Yes, the teenage years are strange and wonderful at the same time. TJ has the body of a man and the mind of a child, and he doesn't realize what that means and how to deal with it. All he knows is that he's been wronged, and I'm to blame.

When I think back to how I dealt with my parents when I was a teenager and now, being a parent myself, I forget what made me so angry. Perhaps it's a general lack of maturity, or maybe a subconscious case of dumb-ass, but I just don't remember acting the way he does. Maybe that's why I was so distant from my father. Hell, maybe that's why TJ and I are so distant. Who knows?

As I look out at the road and the many layers of trees ascending the hillsides, I see what appears to be a green tunnel. The road cuts right through the heart of that tunnel and just keeps on going. The contrast of the natural beauty of the trees being sliced by the man-made road is a bit unsettling. This is truly a metaphor for life because if you think about it, we're all beautiful creatures in our own natural state. Once worldly ideals and pressures come, we're forever changed, and the only way to truly survive is to adapt to the change and surround it, like the trees have done with the road.

I love the outdoors, and I'm grateful that my father taught me to appreciate it. I guess that's the one thing we had in common—maybe the only thing.

I remember when I came home and told my father that I had joined the military. I was eighteen and about one month past my high school graduation. I wasn't able to find steady work, and I really saw no future ahead of me. In my family, we never discussed college, and I didn't think I had what it took to go and find out.

My father's face was beaming with pride for about twenty seconds because that's when I told him I was going to be a Marine. My father was a veteran of WWII and the Air Force, and he thought all other branches of the military were good but that none compared to what the Air Force could do. He was excited about my joining the military because he knew that it could make a man out of me, but he didn't like that I was going to be a Marine.

"What? The Marines? Are you crazy?" he yelled. "Why in the hell would you go and join the damn Marines? Why?"

"I looked at the options, and it seemed to be the best fit for me."

"How do you know what's the best fit for you? You can't even take the garbage out when you're supposed to," he yelled back. "I can't believe this. Wait a damn minute, I see what's going on here—you joined the Marines just to spite me, didn't you?"

"What? No, I... I didn't. It's not about you."

"Oh yes, you don't fool me a bit. You know how I feel about the different branches of the service, and you've heard me say a thousand times that all Marines are arrogant assholes who think they are better than everyone else. So, what do you go and do? You join them! I guess that says a lot about you!" he shouted.

"No, you're wrong. That's not why I did it. I did it for me because it's what I want."

"Go away and leave me alone. I don't want to be around you right now," he said as he sat down in his leather easy chair and blankly stared at the television.

Yes, that was my father, the great encourager. I don't blame him for how my life turned out because my life hasn't been all that bad, but I did most of it alone with hardly any guidance from him.

If I'm being completely honest, there really was a part of me that joined the Marine Corps to spite him, although I never admitted it to him. It was the best decision I ever made because for the first time, I was doing something for me and taking my first step toward manhood.

As hard as he tried to stay angry, I remember my father being there at my graduation from Parris Island. He had softened on his stance, and I think he had begun to see that I was finally becoming a man. I also think he respected me for doing what I did and joining the Corps, although he would never admit it either.

As I gather my thoughts, I look over at TJ sleeping so peacefully in his seat, and I can't help but think of how he reminds me of myself at his age. I used to think that it was cute, but now, I'm not so sure that it's a good thing.

When TJ was first born, it was so amazing. Jen and I had no clue what we were in for, and we had no idea what we were doing. But, we were so happy. She had a difficult pregnancy, and we were constantly worried that something bad was going to happen.

I was convinced that we would have a girl to pay me back for all my misdeeds, but Jen was convinced it was a boy from day one. She never swayed from her conviction as all the symptoms and relatives said it was going to be a girl. Jen had such an—*I told you so*—look on her face when TJ was born. Friends and family would ask how she was so sure, and she would look them in the eye and calmly say, "He had a presence about him, and I could feel his strength. It reminded me of Tom, so I just knew it had to be a boy." Personally, I don't know if she's ever given me such a great compliment.

Those first six or seven years were the best. I would come home from work, and he would run to me with his arms open wide yelling, "Daddy!" He would leap up into my arms before I could put anything down and give me the best hug.

TJ and I would play endlessly, and he was my little buddy. Jen would even complain sometimes that boys were supposed to be closer to their mothers than they were their fathers. I didn't mind because it was the kind of relationship that I never had with my father, and I wanted to make sure that I did it differently with TJ.

Around his eighth or ninth birthday, everything started to change. He was constantly getting into things, and I constantly had to correct or punish him. I must have said, "No," a million times or more those next few years, and every time I said, "No," I became more frustrated with him.

We slowly began to drift apart as he wanted to spend more and more time alone, and it was better that way because it was a hell of a lot more peaceful around the house. Honestly, I had no idea what to do with him, and quite frankly, I still don't.

Sure, we can exist together on some level, but we have no relationship to speak of and no mutual respect. Don't get me wrong, I'm here for him, and I make damn sure that he and all his neighborhood buddies show respect to me and to others. But on an emotional level, we have nothing that works.

He knows I love him, but I'm starting to question if that's enough. Somehow, I don't believe that it is. My father loved me too, but that doesn't mean I spent my adult life in a good relationship with him. My father was a hard man to love. When I look at TJ and all the crap he's going through, I think to myself that maybe he thinks I'm a hard man to love too.

I honestly don't know when the transformation actually happens. Maybe as our children hit their tenth year, they start to put things together, and we, as adults, get into big trouble. I'm totally convinced that once TJ reached an accountable age where he knew what people were all about and he was learning things quickly, he started to pull away from his mother and me—mainly from me. When he was little, I was the king of his world, and I could do no wrong. The playing and the laughing—all of it was what he needed to feel secure and loved.

TJ looked at me with those big brown eyes and trusted me completely. It was as if his whole person would scream, *Wait! Stop everything because my daddy's home. He's gone when I get up in the morning, but I know he'll be here for me later.* Man, I miss those times!

One day, a switch went on inside TJ's head, and he realized that I wasn't perfect. I had many flaws that were blatantly obvious, and he called me on them. Actually, I had no comeback for him, and this is why I think I became so frustrated. He knew me better than anyone and held me on a pedestal, and all I could do was get mad and make excuses.

I look at my son now, and I see the pain and displeasure he has for me when he looks at me. It's like I've let him down or something. I've tried so hard to make sure that I did things differently. I always said that if I had kids, I would do my damnedest to make sure that they never gave me that look; yet, here I am.

I just don't understand. I've been strong in my convictions and beliefs, and I've tried to hold my emotions in check and not let TJ see my weakness. I've tried to not let him see me tear up and get emotionally upset, and I think I've done a good job with that. I'm certainly not perfect, but I think I'm a good father to my son.

As night begins to take over the sky, I reach over and put my hand on TJ, and for a moment, I get to touch my son and connect with him. Shortly after, he wakes up and begins to look around.

"Where are we?" TJ asked as he rubs his eyes.

"We're about two hours away from Ashwell. You hungry?"

"Yes, very."

"Well, there's a restaurant in about twenty miles or so, and we'll stop there. Did you have a good rest?"

"It was okay, I guess," TJ said, not divulging too much information.

"Good, because we have a lot going on in the next few weeks, and you're going to need it."

3

As the road begins to disappear, I notice the cabins as they come into view. The drive has been long and we are both very tired. I pull into the main cabin and walk through the entrance to the front desk. My bones crack as I move, and my knees begin to ache from being sustained in a single position for so long.

I don't remember the exact day that I officially became old, but I think it happened one night when I was twenty-seven. I just remember rolling out of bed, and things hurt—and kept hurting for several days later. I guess it was about that time that I also started to notice the new-found rolls along my waistline.

I sign in and get the keys to Cabin Two. I pay for three months in advance, which seems so strange to me because I've never done anything like this before. On the way back to the car, it hits me—since we've been married, I've never been away from Jen for so long either. I've been in training classes and on other fishing trips but never for more than a week at a time. I guess that after sixteen years of marriage, she needs a break from me—from us.

As I get back in the car and glance over at TJ, I see that his anger has returned, and he is having thoughts of the 'lost summer' ahead of us. I'm sure he would probably say the 'stolen summer,' but I won't press him on it. Now that we're here and he sees the reality of it all, he's feeling trapped.

"We're in Cabin Two, up this road, around the corner—lakeside, I'm pretty sure."

After a period of no answer, I realize that I'm getting the silent treatment again, so I resort to my own little game. I figure I won't let it affect me, and I go ahead and have the conversation with myself.

"That's great Dad. I can't wait to get started," I said in my best TJ voice.

"Now, Son, don't get too excited because there will be plenty of time to experience it all as we go. Don't try to do too much the first week."

"But Dad, I want to…"

"I get it okay," TJ interrupted. "You don't have to mock me, and you know I hate it when you do that."

"Ah, he speaks. Well, at least you finally said something. Between the restaurant and the last two hours of driving, you've said nothing."

"So? Can't I just keep to myself and not have to entertain you?" TJ countered sharply.

"Why do you have to be so damned inconsiderate? I didn't raise you to be a smart-ass kid," my voice becoming a little louder and deeper.

"You didn't raise me," TJ mumbled under his breath.

"What? What did you say?"

"Nothing."

I'm so angry that I almost stop the car and make him get out. I clutch the wheel with a firm grip to keep from unleashing on him. Somewhere deep inside, something is holding me back from doing anything, so I just stare straight ahead and keep driving up the road. This voice keeps calling to me telling me that if I do something, I will only be justifying his anger. I will only be the loudest and the strongest, not the one who is right.

I did hear what he said, and I'm horrified to hear those words coming out of his mouth! *I didn't raise him.* How can he say such a thing? That hurts.

I pull the car into the drive and look up at our home for the summer, and although it's dark, I can see the moon shining off the water. The moon is full and its reflection on the water is a beautiful white glow. I stop for a moment to take it in, and it helps calm me down.

"I'll open the door and get the lights. You start unloading the car."

"Dad," TJ said.

"Just unload the car, and let's get settled."

TJ, his face showing the hurt, turns away. I think he was going to apologize, but I am not at a place to hear it. He just can't say things like that and expect everything to be fine. Sometimes, you've got to think before you speak.

We settle in that evening and barely speak to each other. I don't know what to say to him or how to reach him. All we do is argue, and when we do find a peaceful moment, it's often ruined by something or someone else. Truth is, I really don't want to talk with him.

I wake up the next morning and head out to see Ashwell. I also want to stop and make friends with locals if possible. I leave TJ sleeping in his room. I guess I could have gotten him up, but I need to be alone.

I turn my sights on getting our necessary equipment—things like bait, gas, and maps of the lake. I must admit that I'm a little intimidated by the whole scene. The lake is huge, and if you didn't know any better, you would think you were at the beach, near the ocean. Fortunately, Earl had prepared me for the massive size of it all, but he didn't do the setting justice. The water is an unusual blue-green mix that looks like a shiny emerald when the sunlight hits it just right. The shorelines are pristine and the sand is golden-white, like the color of wheat. The town is well-kept and clean. I can't wait for the afternoon when dusk approaches because, to me, there is nothing more beautiful than a warm, peaceful day near the water when the sun starts to go down. At that moment, my heart relishes the purity and God-like existence of nature and all that she offers.

Heading into The Corner Store, I overhear several locals talking about the weather and other pertinent fishing news. I introduce myself to the skeptical, observant eyes carefully watching my moves.

"Hello. My name is Tom Phillips, and I'm here with my son this summer on a father-son fishing trip. How are you?"

"Well, Tom, glad to meet you," said a loud, booming voice from behind me. "I'm Jim Sanders, and this is Billy, John, and Mike. We sure hope you have a great time this summer up here in our neck of the woods. It's God's country up here, y'know?" he said with a smile.

"From what I've seen this morning, you may be right."

When I was growing up, my father taught me two very important lessons about fishing and fishermen. It was his belief that if you lived by these lessons, you would never get off-course.

First, he would say that fishermen, no matter how friendly on the shore, would never be honest with you about what they caught and where they caught them. Of course, I found through my own fishing experience that there is an exception to that rule. As with anything, there is always a trust factor involved, and fishermen are no different. I've found that if you sit down and eat with them, preferably at a fish fry, then you become an accepted friend and fishing buddy—especially if you share what you caught.

Next, my father always said that your best friend at any lake is the guy who runs the local store where you buy your supplies. His belief was that the storeowner was 'one of the boys' but that it was in his best interest to give you valuable information so you would keep coming back. Sure, all the other guys were getting the same information, and they all knew where it was coming from. But the practice was accepted, and nobody complained. It's like a bartender who knows vital information and is willing to give it, but he does so very carefully and in secret.

"Guys, I appreciate your well-wishes, and I would really like to bring my son to a good, old-fashioned fish fry. You all know of any that are happening soon?"

"Well, we're planning one next Friday night at Mason's boat dock, and you both are definitely invited. Usually, the community gets together about every week and has one at different spots around town," John answered.

"Great! We'll be there. Well, I'm going in to get some supplies. Who owns the store?"

"That's Fred. He's inside working the counter," Mike replied.

"Thanks."

As I enter the store, I have *déjà vu*, as they say, all over again. The shelves are stocked with all the latest lures, worms, sinkers, and floats. Off to the right is a long wooden container full of live minnows ready to be grabbed by a small strainer sticking out of the top. I am eight years old again, and this store is exactly the same as the one my father used to take me to when we went fishing. I pause a few moments to take it in, hear the familiar sounds, and smell the smells of the past.

Fred's store is the kind of place where you can get whatever you need for an all-day fishing expedition. He has plastic worms, crickets, lures, and all sorts of other items only the true fisherman can appreciate. You can even stock up on the essential fishing trip cuisine—cupcakes and donuts, canned sausage and crackers, and finally, beef jerky. To wash it all down, you have to have a thermos full of hot coffee, some cold sodas for the afternoon, and beer to end the day. Ah, yes, no fishing trip is ever truly complete without these essentials.

"How's it going, friend?" comes a voice from behind the counter, all indications saying it was Fred.

"It's good. You?"

"Fine. Just fine," Fred replied. "Did I hear you say that you're here for the summer with your son?"

Fred is a short, older gentleman with a kind smile. At first glance, anyone can tell that his heart is warm and his words genuine. His silver hair says that he's been around a long time and seen many things. His face shows he is someone you can trust.

"Yes, we came in last night."

"What brought you here to Ashwell?" Fred asked as he gives me the once-over review.

"Well, to be honest, I love to fish, and I needed a break from the world. My good friend told me about this place and said that I haven't lived until I've fished for, caught, and eaten a yellow perch. I honestly have no idea if he's right or not, but I figured what the hell, I'd give it a try."

"Then, friend, I would say you've come to the right place, and I think you've got a pretty smart friend, too," he said. "By the way, my name's Fred."

"Fred, great to meet you. I'm Tom—Tom Phillips."

After looking around the store for a few minutes and picking out several essentials, I stop on the aisle with the lures. Apparently, Fred can see my hesitation and offers his assistance. Little does he know that I'm testing my theory on him. He falls for the bait.

"Tom, you mentioned before that you'd never fished for yellow perch, correct?" Fred asked. "Well, let me get you started on a couple of things that'll help."

"That'd be great. What do you have?"

"The others would probably kill me for telling you this, but since you're new here, I'll make an exception," Fred said cautiously looking over his shoulder to make sure he isn't being overheard. "Yellow perch are special, and you must respect that. Unlike most fish, legend has it, the yellow perch are family-oriented separatists that travel in schools."

"That seems like a contradiction."

"Exactly, which is why they're special. From what's been told through the years, the yellow perch will travel in schools like most fish, but the difference is that when they group together, they do so in a family way," Fred explained. "A sense of family and reliable routine are key factors for the yellow perch."

I have to admit that I'm a reasonably good fisherman, and I've heard a lot of fish stories in my life. But I have absolutely no idea what the hell Fred is talking about. He is, however, very serious about it, and I at least owe him my respect to listen.

Fred continued, "For instance, they generally will start biting in early April and go until mid-May. Then, they bite off and on for days throughout the summer, but by that time, they are usually a lot deeper than normal.

"Funny thing though—this year, winter was a lot colder than normal, and I think it pushed them deeper than in the past. They haven't really started biting yet. That's expected to change this week."

"Really, that's good to hear because my friend told me everything he knew about them, and he said I might be too late. Is there anything special used to catch them? I was going to try live minnows or wall crawlers, but I'm not sure."

"Those will work for sure, and if you ask anyone around here, that's what they'll tell you to use. For my money, I would use the silver cyclone," Fred answered. "It does two things the others can't. First, it zigs and zags underwater a little faster than a live minnow does. Next, and more importantly, the silver tail reflects the sunlight, and this makes the yellow perch go crazy."

Fred goes on to show me the different fishing spots around the islands of the lake as we look at the map. He tells me the best place I can go to put my boat in the water. He even says that Mike might have an extra slip I can use for the summer. I ask him about the fish fry and directions to Mason's boat dock, and he tells me that I won't want to miss it.

"Fred, I really appreciate the information, and I'm sure I'll see you everyday."

"Hope so," said Fred.

As I leave Fred's store, I can't help but think about how the world would be a much better place with more people like Fred in it. He's a genuinely good man—the real deal—and he treats everyone with the same kindness and respect that we all want.

When I return to the cabin, I find TJ just sitting around. It looks as if he's just gotten out of bed.

"TJ, I'm planning to take the boat out this afternoon and explore the lake. I got a map and some other supplies from the store down the road. Would you like to go with me?"

"Nah," TJ answered quickly. "Don't think so. Don't really want to."

I think about tearing into him for his crappy attitude, but we just went through this same stuff last night. Honestly, I just don't care anymore what he does, and it's obvious he's shutting me out. If that's the case, then so be it.

"Fine. I'll go by myself. By the way, there's a fish fry on Friday night up the street, and some nice guys I met this morning invited us. Plan on going."

"Okay," TJ said agreeably.

I'll be damned. The little bastard makes me so mad sometimes. I think his goal in life is to piss me off, and he does a great job of it. He just digs and digs until I start to blow. I guess that's what he wants. Who the hell knows?

"Well, I'm gone and you keep your butt around here. I'll be back before dinner."

"Sure," TJ replied.

I take the boat down to Mason's boat dock and put it in the water. I want to casually work my way around the areas that Fred told me about and get a feel for the lake itself. I've never been on any lake this size before, and I always make a quick run before I fish anywhere. To me, there is no sense in just being stupid. Preparation is always the key.

The water is calm and there's a slight breeze in the air. Fortunately, April is a great month temperature-wise, as the sun is warm, but not hot. Even in the afternoon, the heat isn't unbearable. The only thing you really need to be careful of on a lake like this is a sudden storm that can catch you off-guard and mess up your day.

The lake is magnificent. All the stuff Earl talked about it is true. The water is an ocean-like blue-green, and both the mainland and islands have clean, sandy beaches. As I drive my boat around the various coves, I can't help but take a moment to soak up the fading sun on my face. How I love the lake at dusk!

**4** AFTER A WEEK, THINGS BEGIN TO GET A LITTLE
better between TJ and me. Those first few days were
tough because he didn't leave the cabin and had no
interest in fishing with me. I figured the time alone
would benefit us both, and it did.

I must admit that this is a new approach for me in dealing with my
son. Before, I would have made him go out on the lake with me, and we
both would have suffered. I figured that it couldn't get much worse, so
why not give him some space? Amazingly, he responded, and I learned
something.

He decides to go with me to the fish fry Friday night, and we taste
yellow perch for the first time. I consider myself an avid fisherman, and
I have tasted many types of fish before. But I have never tasted anything
so delicious in my life. The batter is golden brown and not too heavy.
The sweet twinge on the side of my tongue, from that first bite, makes
my mouth water for more.

We eat until our stomachs are full and sore, but it is worth every
minute and every bite. TJ and I talk with and meet many of the locals.
Everyone in town is friendly and inviting, so we feel right at home.

Shortly after, TJ finds a renewed interest in going fishing, and we
begin exploring new areas of the lake for the much sought-after yellow

perch. We even plot other areas of the lake where we have been told are good spots. Thus, we begin our summer routine.

We get up early in the morning, about an hour before the sun comes up. We make breakfast, fill the thermos with coffee, and head down to the boat dock to start the day. Fortunately, our new friend Mike knows George Mason, owner of the boat dock, and he has arranged for us to keep our boat in an extra slip he has available for the summer.

We get to the first spot around six forty-five in the morning, just as the sun is beginning to rise, and we fish quietly for two hours. Depending on our luck, we scuttle from one fishing area to another trying to find any hungry school of fish we can. Around eleven, we begin to head back to the cabin to eat lunch and rest because by that time, the day is usually way too hot, and the fish aren't biting.

When three o'clock rolls around, we get up from our naps, start out for The Corner Store to learn the latest news from Fred, and stock up on supplies for the evening and next day. By four-thirty, we're back at the most productive sites trying to catch as many fish as possible. We stay out on the lake in the warm afternoon sun peacefully watching the rays glimmer off the calm, still water. At seven, we're back at the dock putting the boat up and slowly making our way to the cabin to make plans for dinner.

By Tuesday, TJ finally has to ask, "Dad, why do you like being on the lake at dusk? You always say how much you love it, and you can see it on your face when we're out there."

"Well, when I was your age, things seemed to always be so hectic, and the only peace I found was going out to the lake and fishing. After a while, I started to notice that when the sun hit the water just right, the reflection was so inviting that it made my mind drift off to a better place.

"I was also able to come to grips with myself and who I was. Although the process was long, I was able to look into my soul and find myself. I guess I'm just reminded of that journey every time I see the sun glisten off the water."

"Well, I'm just curious, but I don't see it. I'm glad it works for you though."

I don't really want to tell TJ that the reason things were so hectic was because my father was so demanding and generally a royal pain in the ass or that I tried to stay away from him as much as possible. Heck, it's not all bad because I didn't lie to him about the 'why' part of it.

That afternoon, as we're heading around to fish the point closest to the small channel, TJ hits me with a loaded question, and I'm not ready for it.

"Dad?" asked TJ.

"Yes."

"Was Granddad a racist?"

"Um… Well…why do you ask something like that?"

"I saw how he treated people, and I heard what he said about others. To me, there's no doubt about it. I think that he was, and so do my friends."

"Your friends?"

"Yeah, I told them some of the things he said and did. You know that Bill and Charlie both met him and heard him talk about people. We laughed it off, but they never forgot. All my friends believe he was a racist, and I'm just curious what you think."

"Well…"

I begin the sentence, but I honestly don't know if my father was a racist or not. I guess I haven't really ever thought about it too much, so

I'm probably not the best person for him to ask. Okay, so maybe that's a lie. I have thought about it and have formed some ideas, but I don't know which is worse, the truth or the perception.

Growing up, we all knew where our father stood on different issues. Almost to a fault, and even sometimes beyond, he let it be known what he thought. He had grown up in a different time from us, and his world changed. His only defense was to lash out at those who were different from him because he didn't know any other way to do things.

We heard the racial slurs and were told of different stereotypes almost daily—so much so that we could be heard repeating those same phrases in school and among our friends. If you wanted to get on my father's good side, then all you had to do was tell him a good racial joke, and he would just laugh and laugh. As I got older, I really didn't know any better. My father had helped mold me into a mindless and thoughtless mouthpiece, and I believed it was all okay. I would repeat those jokes and call those names out of ignorance.

It wasn't until I began to look at my father on a deeper level and realized how he was that I came to discover that most, if not all, of his convictions were sprung from fear and ignorance. Fear that his world had changed; fear of his perception of being powerless to do anything about it; and ignorance of other people and cultures that fed the fear and put him on the defensive. Combine all of this with his combative approach to life, and his defensiveness seemed abusive. But even as I started to uncover this mystery and many others in my life, I still fell into the familiar when I was around him. I guess I just wanted to win his approval and keep the peace.

Although physically I was growing into a man, I was still a lost child as a person, searching for my way and trying to understand it all. That all changed when I stepped off the bus at Parris Island, home of the Marine Corps boot camp, because life as I knew it quickly changed forever.

Boot camp was the hardest thing I had ever done up to that point in my life. The physical side was tough, but I was in fairly good shape and could handle it pretty well. The tough part was the mental aspect and all the mind games that were played on us from the start.

Sgt. Dwight Thompson is the man I credit to this day for molding me into the person I am. If there was an emotion, then I've had it for him. Ultimately, I came to respect, admire, and love him for who he was and what he did for me. Needless to say, it didn't start out as any of those things; it was pure hate in the beginning, and I have no regrets in saying that.

Sgt. Thompson was a big man—six feet, six inches—and had muscles bulging that I didn't even know existed. We young and impressionable recruits quickly learned that we wanted no part of Sgt. Thompson. He could go toe-to-toe with any of us and not think twice about it. He made us do push-ups in the morning, in the afternoon, and at night. If we messed around or if he were just in a bad mood, then he would add a new element—making us do push-ups in large puddles of mud and water. He also made us run mile after mile, building character, as he called it. It made me sick to watch him sit there yelling at us and laughing. I remember that laugh like it was yesterday. It was a hearty yet sarcastic laugh that just pounded in my ears.

The first month I just went through the motions, and I really didn't care about boot camp too much. I was homesick and missing my freedom, but I managed to keep out of Sgt. Thompson's way. Ironically, I heard racial slurs being shouted at all of us. At times I thought I was at home. The slurs would just rain on us from Sgt. Thompson almost to the point where nobody knew what to make of it. I started to believe that Sgt. Thompson and my father were one in the same because he treated us and called us names just like my father would have. I even began to doubt myself and felt that I had been too hard on my father for the way he was.

Then, about eight weeks into my training, Sgt. Thompson ordered me into his office. "Phillips, get your ass in here right now! Don't make me come out there!"

"Yes, Sergeant."

"Close the door," he barked as he stood up and towered over me.

"Yes, Sergeant."

"Phillips, I've been watching you for two months now and you know what I see?" he said.

"No, Sergeant." I knew this was going to be my shining moment because I had really begun to work the system and excel at the drills. Shortly after my first month, I figured out the game that was being played with our minds. I knew the physical stuff was demanding, but it really wasn't that difficult. Besides, I had the physical strength to be very successful. I knew if I were going to win over my commanding officers, I needed to be more mentally prepared. So, this was going to be my moment—the moment Sgt. Thompson praised me for my work.

"I see a snot-nosed punk who grew up thinking he has the right to pass judgment on others just because of the color of their skin, not because he took the time to get to know them and understand who they are. You're a loner, and yes, you excel at all these piss-ant, bullshit drills we do. But what have you learned? I'll tell you what you've learned— not a damn thing. Do you think you will ever succeed in this life all by yourself? Do you think that anyone, regardless of color, will ever trust you in times of battle or whatever comes your way in life—better yet, when you really need them for something?" he yelled.

I was stunned. My shining moment was dogshit. I didn't let Sgt. Thompson see my frustration with him because I didn't want that to deal with as well, so I stood there with a clenched jaw taking my medicine.

"Wake up, Phillips! Whatever shit you learned at home doesn't work in the real world. A man is judged by what's in his heart and the character he finds when he looks down and his back is against the wall. It's what he does next that makes him who he is," Sgt. Thompson said sharply.

"Permission to speak, Sergeant."

"Granted. I've sure as hell got to hear this."

"Sergeant, I've used those same slurs and acted like I have toward others because you've done the same thing, and I figured if you were doing it, then it was okay."

"You thought it was okay?" he questioned. "See, that's the problem with punks like you. You think you know everything and got it all figured out when, really, you've just got shit for brains. Don't act like you know everything. Try listening for a change. I say those things because I want all of your sorry asses to realize that you're all the same. If you go into battle and you don't trust those around you, you will die! And just for the record, trust doesn't come in any other color but red—blood red. Now, get out of my sight and go think about what I said."

I did think about what he said, but it wasn't until some time later that I truly understood what he told me. I went back to visit with him years later, and I told him how much he changed my life. We sat and talked for a long time, and he seemed so much different than when we were in boot camp. Actually, I was different.

"Well, Son, that's a tough question to answer, and I believe it's more complicated than it seems."

"I would think Granddad either was or he wasn't."

"TJ, your grandfather was a complicated man in many ways, but I believe there are things you need to understand before you pass judgment on him."

"So, you think it's okay that he was?"

"Don't start that crap with me. I'm trying to help you understand what he was all about, and it's not easy for me to sit here and admit negative things about my father, so lighten up a little. All I'm saying is that you need to analyze your grandfather and his ways on a couple of levels, because I think your generation is quick to pass judgment."

"Then, tell me, because it seems pretty easy for me to understand."

"Well, for starters, the key to understanding someone like your grandfather or anyone else from that generation is to understand what makes them who they are and then compare those same feelings and issues with what you're going through in your own life today. For example, your grandfather acted the way he did toward others out of ignorance, not true hate, as you believe. This is the same ignorance that you're using now to pass judgment on him by calling him a racist. Don't get me wrong, your grandfather was a mean and cold-hearted son-of-a-bitch, and he caused me to treat people badly, just because they were different. He taught me to be a racist through his own ignorance."

"So, you're telling me that Granddad, who treated people like crap and called them nasty names, was just ignorant? And you, who treat people with respect, are a racist?" TJ asked. "That's the dumbest thing I've ever heard."

Sometimes our children are so smart, and they see things that we don't see or that we refuse to see. TJ has me on the ropes with his question, and I am looking for a way out.

"Son, in our day and time, people will always feel like they are being persecuted in one way or another—it's inevitable. The questions we have to ask ourselves, then, are things like, "Are they right for feeling that way?" or "Did I do something to cause those feelings?" Regardless, not everyone is always going to agree with you, no matter how meaningfully you present it. Sure, this is a part of life that sucks, but there are people in this world that are filled with hate. You can't stop that. The only thing you can do is make sure that you're not one of those people."

"Honestly, Dad, I don't care about those things right now. What I want to know is, are you serious about what you said, or are you covering for granddad?"

"I'm not covering for anyone. I meant what I said, and you need to listen, try to understand it, and let it go."

"Let it go? Dad, cut the shit and be honest with me for a change."

"What did you say to me? How dare you speak to me like that!"

"Dad, tell me the truth!"

"I don't know what you want from me."

"I want you to be honest with me for a change and tell me the truth!"

"I told you!"

"No, you didn't!"

"Yes, I did!"

"Admit what you don't want to face!"

"There's nothing! I told you!"

"Admit it!" TJ screamed.

"Okay, you bastard. My father was a spineless, ignorant racist who loved nobody but himself, and he treated people like shit."

I couldn't believe what I had said. All of these years and for the first time in my life, I had said what I truly believed in my heart about my father. I've known it was true for a long time and privately I had hoped it wasn't, but I knew it was. Now, here I am blurting out things to my son about his grandfather that he didn't need to hear—even if he did bring it up.

As I look up at TJ, he's frozen in place, and he has the look of a frightened little boy. I guess he figures that I'm going to lash out at him for pushing me so hard, and I can see the fear in his eyes. I take a deep breath and gather myself.

"TJ."

"Yes."

"Son, I'm not mad at you."

"You're not?"

"No. You can be pretty tough on me sometimes. I guess you get that from me."

"Dad, if Granddad was a racist and you say you're a racist, then does that make me one, too?"

"No, TJ, it doesn't. I'm not a racist, and you aren't either. I said that about myself because at one point in my life, I was, and I just wanted you to stop asking me about your grandfather. It took me a long time to make the change, but I did it. I just had the misfortune to grow up in an environment that promoted all the wrong things. Fortunately, when I was in the military, I learned a valuable lesson about life and people from a great man.

"That lesson was that a man has to choose his own way in life and that he isn't defined by the color of his skin but by what's in his nature.

A man's heart makes him true. The irony is that we live in a society where race is such a factor; yet, in order to survive, our society should be colorblind. Good men and women have died trying to help us see this, and people like your grandfather have spent a lifetime making it more difficult. As you get older, the choice is yours on how you treat others. Only you will know what's in your heart and how you want to be. The real beauty of it all is that you can change and make it right if you get off track—just like I did."

"I get it," TJ announced proudly.

"Good. Now let's go to the cabin."

5

THE LAST FEW DAYS HAVE BEEN STRANGE FOR ME. TJ and I haven't really spoken about anything important, but things are a little better than they were when we got here.

My original idea of the summer is pretty close to the reality—nothing special, just TJ and me going through the motions as usual—yet TJ caught me off-guard, asking me about my father and putting me on the spot like he did. I guess I hate it and get the most upset when he acts like me.

The season is starting to get into full swing, and the days are getting hotter. The fishing, too, is becoming more of a trial and test of wills as the fish are going deeper to find the cooler water. The time we had spent going from island to island and plotting routes along the channel early on is really starting to pay off, as we have a place to go everyday and usually, we end up catching something.

The standard Friday night routine is also in full swing. TJ and I have really taken up with Mike and the boys, and each Friday night fish fry has become quite the event. TJ always makes sure that we're there on time. I think he likes the comradery of the guys and being around the adult conversations. He's never cautious with his opinions, and I've noticed that we're on different sides when it comes to a variety of issues. I, of course, have to blame his mother for that.

This particular Friday, the conversation has to do with politics and the upcoming August primaries and elections. Since most races are single party on the ballot, the winner of the August primary wins the overall election because he runs unopposed in the fall.

"There's no way in hell I'm voting for Jeff Johnson," said Mike. "He's a son-of-a-bitch and a snake in the grass."

Of course, this brings out a huge roar of laughter from the others, and Jim replied, "Hey, Jeff is my wife's cousin, and he's not all that bad. He's campaigning to give property owners the shoreline rights that they deserve, so why are you on him like that?"

"Jim, now you know damn well that your wife's family is crazy. Bless their hearts, but they're all one nut short of becoming the poster family for Planters' new special mixed nut batch. Mike's right, no way he gets my vote either," said Billy as the table erupts with laughter again and John slaps the table for effect as they all look at Jim.

Jim gets ready to respond with a profanity-laden outburst when I notice him glance at TJ. He holds his tongue, points his finger, and says, "I'll speak with you later about this. You're all lucky the kid is here." Showing him how much they like him and responding as good friends often do, the boys burst into laughter.

As I watch TJ, I can't help but notice how interested he is in the conversation regarding the elections. Up to this point of the night, I hadn't seen him take such an interest in any of the conversations among the group. He has offered his opinion and asked questions, but tonight he's interested in things like why the candidates are taking stances on the issues they are and what it means for the townspeople who vote for them.

Issue after issue, the group conversation goes from one person and candidate to the next. Mike and the boys always have a lot to say, and it seems that everyone has an opinion to share, which sparks even more debate.

As I listen to the guys talk, I find myself drifting, and memories of my childhood come into my mind so clearly. I can see my father talking with his buddies about a councilman, JD Wilisker, who was going door to door to collect money for a community project. In our town, this wasn't an uncommon practice and councilmen were well-respected for making their sales pitches in person. This particular community project was for a youth activity center so the children would be able to have a place to play sports and do other activities. My father believed very strongly in the project and wanted to help in any way possible.

"JD is a great guy, and I believe he has a lot to offer our community," my father told his buddies. "I've listened to his idea, and I've asked him to come to my house and speak with us on Sunday, so I expect all of you to be there."

My father was a well-respected man in our community, so when he requested your presence at anything, you'd attend, and you'd spread the word. He was the kind of person who would spend his entire weekend helping a neighbor build a deck or helping another neighbor replace his roof. He never asked for money in return. He only asked that if he needed a favor, you'd be there.

JD was no fool, and he knew that if he were to get what he wanted, he needed my father's help. When Sunday came, JD was there and a huge crowd had gathered to listen. He was an elegant speaker, and he spent two hours explaining to the townspeople the benefit of a new community center for the 'young people of America' as he called them. He described how he had lined up construction companies and would pass zoning laws through the council to prevent any roadblocks that might occur. My father's friends listened closely to his every word and were swept away by his delivery.

Although my mother was against it, my father put in ten thousand dollars of their savings and made a public speech in show of support for JD's idea. On that one Sunday alone, fifty thousand dollars was collected from my father and his friends, most of whom gave because they trusted my father, not JD.

A couple of weeks later, JD skipped town and was never heard from again. My father was devastated at what had happened and it was several months before he could face his neighbors and friends again. Everyone was nice, but even at eleven years old, I could tell the difference between the nice words and the true feelings. It was several years before my father regained the trust of some of his friends while others never again listened to anything he had to say.

In our house, the bitterness and disdain for JD was great. My father lost more than his money; he lost the respect and trust of his friends and, to some extent, his wife. To her credit, my mother never said, *I told you so,* but my father still knew it to be true. Fortunately, my mother had put her foot down and didn't let him put their entire savings into the scheme, so they still had some of their money left.

In time, the bitterness toward JD became directed at politics in general and ultimately, the Republican Party, since JD was a Republican councilman. Although it came out several months later that JD had huge gambling debts and his home was about to be foreclosed, my father still took his frustrations out on Republicans—not on JD and not on himself.

"Tom," said Billy. "Tom," he said again a little louder interrupting my thoughts.

"Sorry. Yes."

"What do you think about it?"

"About what?"

"About the way our political process works in this country?"

All eyes turn to me looking for what appears to be the divine inspiration that has been missing up to this point of the night. I'm not ready for the question, and as I glance over at TJ, I see that he's staring at me as well, waiting for the answer.

"I believe that money and politics make strange bedfellows. Come to think of it, anything and politics make strange bedfellows."

At this, the whole group roars again with laughter, and Mike speaks up and says, "Well, he's got a good point." The conversation goes on to other things as they each weigh in with more opinions. I look over at TJ, and I can tell my answer didn't please him. He looks away quickly when he catches my eye, pretending to listen to Jim speak, but I get the message.

Sometimes, it's so hard to know the right thing to say or do at the precise time it needs to be said or done, and nobody is pleased all of the time. My problem seems to be in pleasing TJ at least some of the time. When I think we're getting closer, we drift apart. It's a vicious cycle.

I know it would've been great for me to speak of political philosophies that would've had everyone wanting to grasp a small part of my knowledge and also make my son proud. But the reality is that talking politics with five drunk guys that I've known for two months is the best way to lose friendships and get into things you wish you hadn't.

On the drive back to the cabin, TJ barely speaks to me except to mouth a few answers to whatever meaningless questions I ask. I think about mentioning my reasons for not engaging on the political discussion, but at this point, he doesn't care and won't listen anyway.

"Tomorrow is an early day, so sleep well."

"Sure," TJ mumbled as he makes his way into his room.

I spend the greater part of the night in turmoil, not because of my answer to the guys but because I disappointed my son. How do I win a no-win situation like that? I don't know what it is he wants from me. What is it that makes children our biggest supporters and our biggest critics at the same time? Maybe it's the same answer. Who knows us better than those who live with us everyday?

I wish I knew the day when TJ stopped thinking I was perfect. I remember how he used to look at me with those big, brown eyes, and I could just tell that he thought I hung the moon. Sure, I was his world, but for those years, it was so great to think that no matter how bad I could suck at being a person, someone thought I was special.

Then, as if a light switch is flipped on, the truth is told, and no matter how great you are, you become tainted in your children's eyes—a man forever known with flaws and ultimately robbed of all reason and intelligence. I think my biggest flaw has been the neglect in trying to reconnect with my son. It's been too easy for me to not do anything and keep a strained relationship. The hard part is first recognizing the need to make a change and then actually doing it—a task I may be too late in getting to with TJ.

As we take the boat out the next day, I feel it's the best time to talk about the conversations of last night and what happened. If for nothing else, I have to change the image of those cold eyes piercing through me with disappointment.

"Son?"

"Yes."

"I want to talk about last night."

"We already did. It's no big deal."

"No, we haven't talked about it—not like we need to. I need you to understand my side and my beliefs. It's important to me."

"Forget it!"

"No, I'm not going to."

"Dad, it's not important anymore. If you had something to say, you could have said it last night. I'm really over it now."

"You can be a real ass sometimes. Do you know that?"

"I wonder where I get that from?!"

"Fair enough, but there are a couple of things you need to understand. First, you don't know everything, even though you think you do. Second, you never discuss politics with five drunk guys you've only known for a couple of months."

I can tell by the scowl on his face that he doesn't like what I have to say, but honestly, that's nothing new. I feel this is a good time to let him know what I believe, and realistically, where can he go?

"There are two types of politics in our society: politics of reason and politics of perception. Unfortunately, the perceived reality is what's usually followed, not the true, heart-felt belief that we each feel and possess. Politics of reason is the basic, fundamental principle where you look at everything objectively and logically, and then you decide which is the best path to follow. That's it, plain and simple. You have to follow your own core value system. Politics of perception has you believe the rhetoric of one discipline or another, and your individualism gets sold to the highest bidder or to the church of popular opinion, not your own."

I can see the wheels slowly turning in his mind because his ignorant dad has made him think. I've never proclaimed to be a well educated man, but I do know what I believe and where I stand on the issues. I guess I shouldn't take pride in the fact that I made him think a little bit or the fact that he might actually recognize that I'm not as stupid as he thinks I am, but I do anyway.

"Sure, Dad, all of that sounds great, but how do you explain people begging for food, people having their rights violated, and people destroying the air we breathe?" TJ inquired. "If I'm completely honest, those are the things that I'm concerned about."

"Well, I would certainly hope that you would be."

I can tell that TJ is a little surprised by my response, although he'll never openly admit it. He knows that on most things I'm conservative at heart, and I guess he thought I'd take the bait, causing another huge argument like we've always had. It's strange, but not today—I just don't want to go there. Maybe I'm changing because my reactions in the past had never worked, and all of the great points I've made over the years were never heard. Who knows why, but I'm not going to do it today.

"TJ, I don't care if you spend your entire life as a bleeding heart liberal, and we clash on everything from today until the end of time. But I want you to remember these two things: First, you will change as you grow older and life slaps you around a few times; and second, if you're going to be a bleeding heart, then by God, be the best damn one you can be. Don't half-ass it and fumble your way through life. If you have a belief you feel is true, then follow it through to the core, whichever side of the fence you find yourself on."

The look of shock on his face is priceless enough, and the lack of response at least lets me know that I've gotten through at some level—whether or not it will sink in is still a mystery.

"Son, when I talk about politics of perception and how minds are molded through inclusion and fear, that's what I'm talking about. Don't come to me with blatant rhetoric that somebody said years ago because now it's a good sound bite. Come to me with original thought and ideas that bring about change, both for you and for society.

"I was like you once. I followed my friends, and out of spite, I went against my father's beliefs and fell headfirst into the conservative way of life. Granted, I still follow a lot of those conservative principles today, but I'm more open and honest about ideas different from mine than I ever have been. I came up with the politics of reason idea because it was the only thing I found that described my rescue from unhealthy perceptions. I don't have all the answers, and I probably never will, but I at least have the comfort of knowing that I've examined the issues. I know that my beliefs are not my father's, my friends', or anyone else's but mine. They're logical, caring, and real if to nobody but me. I just want you to do the same thing—find your own answers and then experience the peace that comes with understanding. You can start now, and as life happens, you can grow and process it for what it is—true reason."

TJ and I spend the rest of the day fishing in our designated areas. Our conversations are casual and otherwise meaningless on the larger scale. I believe that my words have gotten through to him because his facial expressions show that he's thinking and processing what we've discussed. I expected more questions from him, but all I received was silence. Slowly, I begin to question if I've done the right thing, and now, I'm starting to believe that I might have alienated him even more.

The irony is that I've felt like saying those words to him for so long, but when he starts his bleeding heart stuff, we get nowhere because I respond with the same rhetorical slogans and ideas that I learned in my early introduction into conservative thought. It's truly liberating to tell him how I feel and what I believe. For so long, we've been on the wrong side of the mirror looking out, and we've drifted so far apart that at times, I've questioned whether we can ever get it back. I still don't know for sure.

Later that night, I'm caught by surprise when TJ speaks. I guess I've grown accustomed to the silence, and I've spent the majority of the evening reflecting on my own behavior.

"Dad," TJ said.

"Yes."

"I heard what you said earlier, and I've thought about it. How do you ever really know what is right?" TJ asked. "I mean, it seems that people spend their whole lives following a belief or an ideal, and in reality, they may be wrong."

I'm so proud of TJ right now because for the first time in his life, he is thinking about things so much deeper than ever before. Hopefully, he will use this as the makings of something good and strong in his life, something to build upon.

"Son, there is no right or wrong when it comes to politics and which way you choose. The truth isn't always black or white. Trust me, it's hard for me to say that since I've spent most of my life living in a black and white world. I've been in the middle of it and studied for a long time, and the best answer I can give you is politics of reason. I believe that if you understand and break the political structure down to its core, then take that knowledge—apply logic, reason, and feeling to it—you'll come up with your beliefs."

"But how do you break it down and make it easy to understand? There's so much to know."

"I believe any political system such as ours can be broken down into two parts—fiscal and social politics. Under these two headings, you can put all other categories and break them down one by one. For example, on the fiscal side, there are two areas that I hold true as my core—taxes and capital industry."

I can tell that he doesn't understand what I mean and that I'm assuming things he doesn't know or hasn't been exposed to.

"Let me give you an example of what I'm talking about regarding taxes. Broken down to its basic core, we would both agree that in some form, all Americans should pay taxes, correct?"

"Yes."

"Well, given that understanding, the question becomes this…Do you believe that you're going to both save more and spend more of your leftover income if I increase your taxes and take more from you each month?"

"I don't know."

"The question doesn't have to be answered today, tomorrow, or for a while in your case, but it's an essential answer that one day you'll need to be ready to defend, whatever you decide. For me, there is no issue here because if I give more to pay my taxes, then I'll spend less on buying 'fun' things. If I spend less and those around me spend less too, then consumer goods aren't bought, manufacturing stops, jobs are lost, and the economy goes into a recession."

"I've never thought of it like that."

"Well, this is my opinion and my belief that I hold true. I'm not saying it's right, just that I believe it. Someone else may say that the additional money taken from my taxes goes to the government and is allocated to build new roads, fund jobs for teachers, and promote universal healthcare options for those less fortunate. As I said before, there is no right answer, only what we individually hold true."

"I think I see what you mean. I guess it works the same for the social side as well?"

"It sure does, and it gets even trickier sometimes because emotions and feelings get hurt a lot more."

TJ and I spend most of the night talking about which issues belong on the fiscal side and which issues belong on the social side of the political landscape. We debate and, for a change, take the other's stance, arguing against what we believe. We laugh a lot, and I think we connect a little.

6

TJ AND I CONTINUE OUR DISCUSSIONS FOR DAYS after with our newfound sense of understanding that we've discovered about each other. Our debates are lively, and I so enjoy watching his mind work and draw new conclusions.

It's fun for me to participate, as TJ presents his argument and stands firm in his opinions. Then, I offer him, whether I believe it or not, an alternative view of what he thinks and has just presented. My motivation is not only to try and mess with his mind but also to let him be exposed to the other side for a change.

To my surprise, I find myself taking pride in the depth of my son's convictions and his willingness to look at other alternatives. This is the first time I've ever seen him truly contemplate life. His arguments are sharp—his relentlessness unquestioned—but he's still very guarded with his emotions. I guess I can't blame him too much, as I'm doing the same thing to him. Let's face it—how do you act? I've had virtually no relationship to speak of with my son for years. Now here we are, hundreds of miles from home, stumbling around trying to make it through the summer without killing each other, and we find a common, safe ground to connect. Now we have a chance to build on this momentum and move forward. But how? Scary? You're damn right it's scary! I have no idea what to do.

At the midpoint of our trip, both TJ and I are pretty close to becoming locals. Once we learned the right places to fish, we became very good at catching the prized yellow perch, sharing our harvest at the fish fries and talking about everything there is to talk about with the boys. Our routine is simple and our existence, even more so. I can't believe that we've gone more than two months without turning on a television. Of course, TJ was upset at first, but I think he has begun to enjoy the quiet and the calm.

When Monday arrives, I have a surprise in store for TJ. He's up and ready to get going on our normal routine, so we start the morning drive. This time, he knows something is going on when I pass the boat dock.

"Dad?" TJ asked.

"Yes."

"What's up? We just passed the dock."

"Well, today we're doing something different, and I wanted to surprise you."

"What is it?"

"Today, we're taking a charter boat out to see how the professionals' fish, and we even get to participate, too."

"Cool...sounds like fun!"

Hold on a damn minute—is this my son? I don't think he's said he thought something was going to be fun in about ten years. I have to say, I like the sound of it. Maybe we're getting somewhere. Maybe there is still hope.

Bob Wilson and his crew of two are waiting for us as we approach his boat, and what a beautiful boat it is. *Old Number 7* is forty-five feet long and has a purring engine that would make any mechanic blush. The one part of the boat that stands out, other than the size, is the fishing chair, appropriately called *The Big One*. The chair has a huge rod and reel attached to its base and a concoction of belts, latches, and harnesses that would make any astronaut jealous.

Bob had finished painting his boat a few weeks before when I ran into him at the Friday fish fry. He was sitting close to my table, and I leaned over to introduce myself since I didn't recognize his face. He told me he had been away for about a month getting his boat refinished. That, of course, led to a discussion about the boat, and from there, he invited TJ and me to fish with him.

TJ wasn't around when I had talked with Bob and made plans for the big adventure. He was busy trying to learn more about a certain young lady in town, Penny Roberts. I learned later that he had spotted her working once when we visited the theme park and then again one other Friday night. Apparently, she likes TJ as well, because it seems like the two of them are together a lot, and I almost always have to go find him when it's time to leave. He, of course, gives me very little details about her. He introduced me to her once for a brief instant before they disappeared again.

As we leave the dock, a cool mist is hovering above the water as the sun begins to rise in the sky. Having grown accustomed to the weather patterns, I know this is going to be a very hot day. I've made up my mind that today is going to be about TJ, and I want him to experience this first-hand.

I sit with Bob throughout most of the morning. We drink our coffee and talk about the town, the people, and the fishing. He tells me stories from the past and how difficult it is to run a charter fishing boat on a fresh water lake. He says he's given it up twice before but that he continues to be drawn to it. The lake is his flame—it's in his blood—and he knows he'll never leave.

"Tom, it's tough to get by sometimes, but I tell you, I wouldn't trade it for anything," Bob said.

"I imagine so. Do you stay busy?"

"During the summer, we're pretty busy with repeat business. It's tough because most people's first reaction is like yours—disbelief."

"I didn't…"

"Don't worry about it. It was written on your face. Tom, the secret is in the adventure. Who cares if it's fresh water or not? The beauty is in the experience. You sit in that chair one time and fish, then you'll know."

Bob's two crewmembers are his sons, Luke and Joe, ages nineteen and seventeen respectively. One is still trying to find himself and the other, still trying to finish high school. He spares no details in telling me the many trials they've each put him through over the years, yet his voice is affectionate and caring as he speaks. He pulls out a map and shows me a part of the lake I've been curious about but have been too afraid to try in my boat. He explains that there are many perils that lurk in the lake and that I'm wise for not trying that particular area. Bob is very candid in what he says to me about the area and the people. He seems to generally love where he is in his life, and he's at peace with himself.

After lunch, TJ is fastened into *The Big One* and is ready to make his mark on the fishing world. Fortunately for him, Bob's two sons are close enough to his age that he feels comfortable with their advice and encouragement, so he decides to try something new.

I sit back in my shaded co-pilot seat and watch as my son throws his line out and begins to fish. I notice where his body is tanned to a golden brown by the many days of sun we've experienced. His muscles are working hard, and I can see the ripples forming on his back and arms. At that moment, it hits me—my son is becoming a man. It's like it happened overnight. He's not the same lanky teenager I left with nor is he the little boy I remember having thousands of conversations with about the color of my truck.

Where does time go? What causes us to go through life stuck in neutral and then wake up one day asking ourselves, "What the hell happened?" I really wish I knew the answer and why I'm on this side asking the question.

As I watch more closely, I can see that TJ's really enjoying himself. It appears that for the first time in his life, he's in control and making decisions on what to do next. He's reacting and feeling his way forward, and he's excited. I leave him alone because too often, I've been the guy who tries to control everything for him. If he doesn't do something right, I step in, or I keep yelling out reminders for him to be careful or to look for certain things that might come up. Today, however, I'm not about to take any of this away from him.

Later that afternoon, as we begin our two-hour ride to shore, I come up and sit down beside him. We had hardly spoken for much of day.

"TJ?"

"Yes."

"Have you had a good day?" I said, as I pull out a soda to have with him.

"I have."

"I'm glad you've had a good time today because it seemed to me like it was something fun to do."

"It really was, Dad. Thanks."

We finish our drinks without saying another word until we reach land. As we sit on the front deck of the boat, we look out as the sun begins to set and the sky has an orange-red hue across the clouds. The clouds remind me of a beautiful snow-capped mountain range full of newly fallen, untouched soft snow. If I had any artistic talent, I would sit here and paint it, so that the scene would forever be captured. It truly is beautiful.

I look at this magnificent scene before me, and then I glance over at TJ. I think to myself—*Wow, two miracles!*

THINGS HAD BEEN GOING GREAT BETWEEN TJ AND me these past few weeks. For the first time, we were talking and spending quality time with each other. But all good things must come to an end, it seems, because before I know it, we're back at it a few days later. I swear, the aliens are driving me nuts with this, and I've cracked a lot of eggshells trying to work my way through it.

I make the comment that God is surely involved in making this town and the beautiful scenery that surrounds it because no man can have this much vision. For some reason, TJ, who woke up in a bad mood, feels it necessary to test me. He knows this drives me crazy and pisses me off; yet, he gets some perverse thrill from it.

"Do you believe in God?" TJ asked.

"Yes, I do. Why?"

"Just curious," he responded quickly. "Are you a Christian?" he asked firmly as his eyes quickly look at me to see how I answer.

"Yes, I am. Why do you keep asking me these questions? What difference does it make one way or the other?"

"I don't know, but you seem to talk about God a lot, and I really don't see where you follow His Will like you should."

"Really?"

"Yes."

I know where this is coming from, and it just makes me madder the more I think about it. No, it isn't from TJ; although, he, for some reason, feels he has the authority to challenge me on a moral level. It's my mother talking through him. Don't get me wrong. I love my mother dearly, but there's one area where she and I have a major disagreement—religion. Ironically, our beliefs aren't as far apart as she would like to believe; it's just that we believe differently on how religion should be approached.

My mother tried for years to get me to go to church with her, and I did go most of the time because I was guilted by the unknown fear of going to Hell. My father only went to keep the peace in the family. From an outward appearance, my family was as God-fearing as they came.

When Jen and I were married and for a while after that, my mother would constantly bring up church. I would sit down and explain to her what I believed, but my beliefs were never treated with any respect, nor were they ever considered. Her mission to save us never stopped, and it became even more aggressive once TJ was born. We were getting church talks that tried to lay fear on our hearts. She would say things like, "He needs that training," or "How will he ever know right from wrong without knowing God?" Each time, the strike would be swift and deep, and we were left standing amazed at how much our voices went unheard.

The pressure and the burden were so heavy. Jen and I would joke about the absurdity of it all and how Sunday School had apparently turned into a seminar on the finest spiritual closing techniques available.

We could just picture the scene in our minds—*Hell and Damnation Workshop: A Salvation Role-play.* "No, Sister Johnson, you need to be more firm and hold your ground; you never stop after the first, 'No,' Brother Nathan would say. "Okay, this time, I want Sister Johnson to be the unrepenting relative and Sister Thomas to be the soul-saver."

It's sad that Jen and I could even joke about such a thing. The irony is that we both truly believe in God and for all that He stands; yet, we're treated and regarded as sinners because we don't attend church on a regular basis. Personally, I don't really have an answer as to how you can overcome such an obstacle in your life when someone you love and respect like your mother believes you're going to Hell; especially, when you believe that you're standing on the same side of the battle that she is, only your view of the battlefield is different from hers.

I have to say that the issue of church and religion has been one of the hardest things to overcome in my life. I've tried for so long to suppress my feelings of hurt and denial about not being heard, and I still haven't found all the answers I'm looking for. Now, just when I think I've made real progress and I'm moving forward, it's all right back at me again.

"You know, TJ, sometimes we don't have the ability to know everything, and things aren't always as clear as they seem. I know you've been enjoying your time at church and going with your grandmother, but you need to be careful about what you say and talking about things you think you know but don't."

"Listen, Dad, I'm smart enough to figure things out for myself, so don't treat me like a child," TJ fired back. "I do like going to church with Grandma, and yes, we've talked a lot about many different things. But I can make my own decisions."

"I'm not saying that you can't or aren't capable of making your own decisions. What I'm saying is that you should be aware of how others believe and the reasons that make them feel the way they do. If you understand those things, then you'll come to know how people are going to behave and react, and that's one of life's best lessons."

I think I'm keeping calm under the circumstances, and for a moment, it appears that TJ understands what I'm saying. But I think it's too much to ask of anyone, much less a fifteen-year-old.

"Dad, it boils down to a pretty simple thing—if you claim to love God and have faith, then why aren't you in church gaining knowledge and being with others who can help you on your way to Heaven?" TJ asked.

A great twist he has me in, or so he thinks. Strangely enough, I can't help myself and give way to a smile as I turn my head before he catches my eye. Although I'm ill at him for continuing his line of questioning, I'm also glad to see his mind expand and learn. I am, however, still pissed about being put on the defensive by my mother, who is using my son to speak her words.

"Son, I used to go to church all the time, and I was a devout, God-fearing Christian. I'm still a Christian and, I would say, devout and God-fearing, but now, I just don't go to church except on occasion."

"That doesn't answer my question, and you know it," TJ said harshly. "I think I deserve to know."

"Well, okay then, if you deserve to know. But, you might not like what you hear."

"I can handle it."

"Fine. As I said before, I used to go to church all the time. Hardly a Sunday would pass when my mother, my sisters, and I would head out to Sunday School and church services. My father would only go on Sunday morning and spent the rest of the time trying to exorcise his own demons. He had such a strong following in the community that he was elected as a deacon in the church and even given special permission to only come to the morning worship service. This made my mother very angry with him because she thought he took advantage of the system and made his own rules. Of course, my father could always make somebody angry, so this was nothing new."

TJ looks up at me, and for a moment, I think I can read his mind. Yeah, actually, I'm sure of it. Keep dreaming, you bastard. I'm not like my father.

"Anyway, our denomination felt that the best way to minister to others was to have a set of doctrines that everyone should follow. By doing so, we would all continue to be 'trained' in the way of the church—at least in the doctrines of our church. When I reached your age, I began to question what made our church any better than the next church, and so forth. My mother met this with resistance because, for her, asking questions meant that her faith was weak. She would tell me that I needed more faith and to pray for strength. Then, she would give me the reasons why we believed what we did—all of which were doctrines from our church, not necessarily doctrines from God."

"I guess she finally changed your mind?"

"No, she didn't, but I didn't keep questioning her about it either because I knew it made her uncomfortable, and I loved her too much to do that to her."

"Do you think Grandma is weak in her faith—or even wrong?"

"No, absolutely not! I believe that your grandmother has great convictions and a true love of God, but I also think her mind isn't as open to new ideas as she believes it is."

"Sure, it's easy to say something like that, but what gives you the authority to say what's right and what's not?"

"Nothing. But what gives you the right to question my faith and beliefs like you did a few moments ago? See, that's what pisses me off about the whole establishment—the fact that you and people like your grandmother can question my faith because you go to church and I don't. Yet, you're no different than anyone else who sits in judgment of others. In fact, you're just like them or maybe even worse because you use the pulpit as your courtroom, and you can take the moral high ground if you're questioned about it.

"You're no different than me. You're no different than anyone else. The fact is that we all have a tendency to judge others, and we all have the belief that we know what's best. All I'm saying is that God is the only judge we should ever have on our faith—not you, not me, not your grandmother, nor anyone else. I don't have all the answers, but I do know that until you question your faith and its existence, you'll never come to fully understand God and your own spirituality. Every man has to go his own way, and whether or not you decide that church is your way doesn't matter in the end. What matters is that you love God, follow His Will, and treat others with the same respect they should treat you."

TJ is listening to me very carefully. I can't determine if it's because he's waiting for me to say something negative about him, my mother, or the church or if he's really listening. Oddly enough, I've never been able to express my true feelings about religion and the church so exactly as I have today. My heart feels liberated to some degree because my burden has been verbalized. My mother, as much as I love her, has pushed me over the edge in using my son to send her message. I won't allow it to happen again, and we will talk.

"So, are those the reasons you stopped going to church?" TJ asked. "I'd really like to know."

"Not entirely. As I just mentioned to you, my reasons for going to church were because of the guilt placed on me through fear. My faith was there, but I had real issues with a single, denominational view of God.

"When I met your mom, she was sixteen, and I was eighteen and about to leave for the Marine Corps. I had already signed up, but not scheduled to leave 'til the end of the summer. We had about three months together before I left, and she agreed to write me while I was gone. It was your mother who really helped me get through it all."

The thought of Jen when she was sixteen years old and looking at her from across the room warms my heart. I remember being so intimidated by her beauty that it took me two hours to get enough nerve to even talk with her. Once I did, I never looked back. I knew she was the one for me.

"So, I guess you're saying that Mom is the reason you left the church," TJ asked sarcastically.

"No, and you need to be careful of accusing your mother of anything. You also need to keep in mind that I've only left the establishment, not the faith. You see, your mother and I had been dating for about a month when she invited me over to meet your grandparents. She warned me that her parents were very religious and devout in their beliefs. They were followers of one denomination, and my family followed another. To me, there was no difference in the two, and at the time, I really didn't think anything about it. The plan was for me to stop by early for about thirty minutes to meet your grandparents, and then your mother and I would go out. I remember your grandma being friendly but reserved. She asked the typical questions of any new boyfriend your mother brought home, but I could tell something wasn't right."

"What did Grandpa do?"

"Well, he didn't even bother to get up from his chair when I came in. I gave him the benefit of the doubt at first because I figured it had to be difficult with his daughter bringing in new boyfriends quite regularly. Then, after about twenty minutes with your grandma, I went to find your grandpa and introduce myself. He was unresponsive and didn't even bother to acknowledge my presence in the room. I left before becoming too angry, and your mother and I had a terrible time."

"That doesn't sound like Grandpa. He's great, and you seem to get along good now."

"Sure, now we get along fine, but at the time, it wasn't fun. It wasn't until later that night that I figured it all out, and I was very upset. Your grandpa judged me without knowing me, and I was so pissed at him that I decided that your mother and I were finished—even though I thought she might be my soul mate."

"What changed your mind? Something had to happen."

I can tell this is getting interesting for TJ. Although he probably wasn't ready to hear the truth like this, he does seem profoundly interested in hearing about his mother and me. I don't want him to feel any negativity toward his grandparents, but he did ask for the truth and sometimes, it hurts.

"Well, Son, something did happen and rather unexpectedly. After about a week of moping around and feeling depressed, my father came into my room and asked me what was going on. I told him what had happened with your grandpa, and he said something I'll never forget. He asked me if I could love your mother, and when I said that I thought I could, he advised me that if I thought she was worth it, then I should look beyond her parents and treat them as obstacles to overcome.

"He also suggested that the problem was with them, not with me.

The fact that they were passing judgment on me was due to my church beliefs and the doctrines I was following. That conflicted with their firm belief that they knew the best way to get to God. He helped me understand that in the end, they would have to answer to God for their judgments and that it was this misconception of the power given by the church that falsely allowed them to behave like they did. Soon after that talk, I called your mother, and we started seeing each other again."

"I guess it wasn't too fun."

"No, it wasn't fun, and it wasn't until I was in the Corps that I understood some things. I had a good friend in the Corps that I got to know very well. His name was Nazr Templeton. Nazr was a devout follower of Islam, and although we had nothing in common in our backgrounds, we developed a strong friendship. We had many conversations about religion and life—me from my perspective, and he from his. We didn't always agree, but the conversations helped me better understand my own situation."

"So, what was it that helped you understand things?"

"Once, I received a letter from your mother, and I was homesick. Nazr could tell I was upset, so he asked me about your mother and how we met. Those questions turned into an in-depth conversation when I told him about your grandpa and how he dismissed me the first time we met. Nazr explained that the paths to Allah, or God, were many and that we each have to find our own way. To this day, that is the most profoundly honest statement of faith anyone has ever spoken to me. Do you understand what it means?"

"No, not really."

"It means that in any faith, we spend entirely too much time worrying about petty, insignificant issues that divide us. We're consumed with the false authority that our religions or denominations have all the answers and the ability to pass unwarranted judgment on others. Essentially, this is why I don't go to church and why I have a problem with its doctrines.

"To me, as Nazr put it so eloquently, God can be found in many different paths, or religions. The fact that I choose to be a Christian and that is my path to God doesn't mean that I have the only truth. Nor does it mean that I should ever believe myself to be better than someone else just because we disagree or because they believe something different. Faith isn't about Jesus, Mohammed, or even Buddha. It's about God. We should all take the time to listen to those with differing ideas, take their truths to heart, and ask questions about our own spirituality. Only then will we find answers."

TJ is looking at me so differently, and I'm looking at him with hope. His mood has softened, and I can tell that the words were not easy for him. But he holds it together like a man. For that, I'm proud.

"TJ, this is my belief. Again, I may not go to church, but I do know my spirituality and my own faith. One day, you have to make your own way and draw your own conclusions. When you do, you will find your true calling and your true faith."

"I get it!"

"Good. Are you hungry? Let's go get something to eat."

8 THE WEEKS HAVE GONE BY FAIRLY QUICKLY. THE TOWN has started to treat us as its adopted children. We know people by name, and we can tell you how many children—aunts, uncles, and others—are in each family. More importantly, we know who the best cooks are. Just thinking about all the desserts at the Friday fish fries makes my mouth water, and it makes me miss Jen even more. Jen is such a great cook, and on my long list of reasons I had for marrying her, her cooking ranked near the top.

As we head up the road to our cabin after a long day, we see the black SUV as we approach. For the first time in more than a week, TJ is smiling. He's smiling so wide that I don't think he's aware of how obvious he is. Actually, I have to admit that I catch myself feeling a little happy when I see Jen's car parked in the driveway of our cabin.

Jen has come to visit us, and it's an unexpected welcome. As I park the car, TJ is out the door before the wheels stop rolling. He runs inside while I make my way around. When I walk through the door, I see TJ and Jen embraced in a big hug. His back is to me, and I can see Jen's smiling face. Her eyes look at me with a curious glance like she's baffled by how much TJ has missed her, but I can tell that she isn't about to let go first.

As I look back at her, I give her my classic grin that I know drives her crazy. For those few seconds, I can feel my heart starting to warm, and my emotions starting to let their guard down. I look away and then say something funny to mask my true feelings—same as I always do.

"Well, are you going to let go of my woman anytime soon? I missed her, too."

"Come here you big stud. Hey, I like the dark tan. I couldn't stay away from my boys any longer, so I thought I'd surprise you." Jen said as she comes across the room to give me a hug.

TJ and I both agree that we're very surprised and glad to see her. "Mom, how long are you staying? The rest of the time, I hope."

"No, no—I'm going back. I have to be back at work on Monday," Jen replied. "Besides, this is a guy trip."

"Well, honey, I'm certainly glad you're here. It will make it even better, and I missed you a lot."

As I say this, I tilt Jen's head back and start kissing her with long, deep kisses that show her that I really did miss her and that I'm very glad she came to see us. TJ, of course, doesn't care much for the public display of affection that we're showing, so he quickly makes his exit to his room. "Great. Do you have to do that in front of me? It's just not a pretty sight. Have some mercy, please."

"Works every time." Jen and I said together as we burst into laughter.

"Yes, it does."

Jen looks so beautiful as we sit on the couch in the living room. Sure, we've spoken on the phone each night, but it's good having her close. The chemistry we have together is so real, and I never realized how strong it was until we were apart. As Jen is telling me about all the things that are going on back home, I drift off to when we were separated this long the last time, which was when I went into the military. I remember it like it was yesterday—especially, now that the circumstances are pretty much the same. Jen and I had been dating for a few months, and I knew it was my luck to find the girl of my dreams and then have to leave.

Boot camp was so mentally hard, and I spent a lot of time thinking about and missing Jen. She was great and wrote me letters every week. Those letters were what helped me stay sane and kept my head up through the insanity. About a month into training, I wrote her and told her that I thought I had made the wrong decision in joining the Corps. I even said that maybe my father was right about me, and that I should've listened to him and joined the Air Force or even done something else with my life. I was missing her—and home—and I wanted somebody to pity me and my situation.

I've never forgotten what she wrote back. Once I got the letter, I couldn't wait to read it. Finally, somebody was going to understand the hell I was in. Only no one told that to Jen.

Dear Tom,

I received your letter the other day, and I don't know what to say. I didn't think it was possible, but I'm extremely disappointed in you. I know you're homesick, and I understand that you'll have doubts about your decision because that's normal. What I don't understand is that after all you've been through with your father, why would you back away from the biggest decision of manhood you've ever made in your life? I know boot camp has to be tough for you and the others, but if you're going to be a Marine, then you need to start acting like one. I am proud of you, and I love you. When you're done, I'll be waiting for you.

Love, Jen

Honestly, that letter changed my life on many levels. I keep it with me every day to remind myself to be a better person. It helped me to become a damn good Marine, and I never pitied myself again. Also, I knew at that moment that I was going to marry Jen and be with her forever because she saw the real me and still didn't care.

Now, as I watch Jen speaking, I feel those same feelings again. I'm so excited that she has come to see us, and I know TJ wants a break from me. This will also give me the chance to go out by myself and think without having to worry if TJ is alright or if he's up to something. Some of my best thinking is done while I'm fishing—it just sort of soothes my soul. Every man needs his alone time, and I'm no different. I seem to get to the place in my life where I believe I can work it out without taking the time to be alone, but I'm wrong. My alone time is the only thing that keeps me true to myself. It's the only time I have for me to look more closely at my good and bad sides and make peace with them.

"Mom, since you're staying through the weekend, you'll get to go to the fish fry on Friday night," TJ said as he entered into the room. "It's great, and the food is awesome."

"Well, sounds good to me," Jen replied.

"Oh, don't let him fool you. He likes the food for sure, but he's sweet on a certain young lady."

"Dad, why do you have to bring that up?" TJ asked sharply.

"Well, it's true, isn't it. I just thought your mom might like to know."

"TJ, honey, don't listen to him. The fish fry sounds like a great idea. How about you and me spend some time together the next few days and have some fun?" Jen asked.

"I'd love to," TJ said as he gives me a quick glance that says he's more than happy to break from our routine—and me—for awhile.

"Before I forget, I spoke with your teachers, and they thought that since you had shown such good potential this year in school, you should be in Advanced Placement courses next year," Jen said. "They said that it'll help you prepare better for the SATs you have to take, so I went ahead and signed you up, okay?"

"Sure," TJ mumbled softly, looking like his worst nightmare had come true.

"TJ, I think it will be good for you. You'll see," Jen said, trying to bring his mood up.

"Yeah, I know—whatever," TJ responded, as he leaves the room.

TJ is bright, and he always shows great potential in school. But when the time comes to excel and move to the next level, he holds back. We have no idea why he doesn't try to push himself harder or what his problem is, but we both wish it would change.

"Honey, just let it go. He's been like this a lot since we've been here. He'll come around. I'll speak with him about it later."

The next few days are wonderful. I go about the same routine that TJ and I have been following from the beginning, but now everything is just quiet—not the silence of someone not speaking to you, but the still, peaceful quiet that we all long to have.

On my third day of fishing alone, the lake has an unusual stillness to it. Surprisingly, there aren't that many boaters, and even the locals aren't fishing as much. Perhaps it's the hot day, but even the fish aren't around. I sit back in my seat and close my eyes as I feel the warm sun on my face. I can hear the water swells splash on the sides of my anchored boat as it rocks back and forth slowly, and my mind drifts into a lazy sleep. Ah, the tranquility of it all! Peace is finally here.

I hear a noise coming from the other end of the boat, and it sounds like someone is going through my tackle box. I immediately come to attention and look to see what it is. To my surprise, my father is sitting in the front seat of the boat getting his pole ready to cast. I rub my eyes to be sure, but he's still there. He smiles at me after a quick glance my way and goes back to what he's doing. For us, fishing always seemed to be our bridge to each other, our communication.

"Bet you didn't think you would see me here again. Well, here I am."

"No, I didn't. This can't be real."

"What is real, Tom? Does it really matter?"

"Always with the attitude. You can never just be nice."

"Tom, lighten up. I think I've lived a lot longer than you have, so I'm entitled to act how I want to act or say what I want to say."

"Whatever."

Most of the time, my father was an ass to me and to everyone around him. Maybe he was unhappy with himself, and he wanted others to feel his pain. Maybe he was just a prick, and he liked making those closest to him miserable. I have to just stop and concentrate for a moment because we're back to arguing again—same as always.

"You know, I hate you sometimes. You make me so mad that I could beat the living shit out of you just to shut you up. Why can't you just be nice to me and treat me with some respect? Why can't you just accept me for who I am, your son? Why do we have to do this same shit over and over?"

"What would it solve? You and I have been doing this crap for years, so why change now?" he asked. "What makes you think you're any different?"

"Oh, I'm different."

"Really? Isn't that nice to know?"

"You bet your ass it is."

"How does your son feel about it? What would he think was different about you? I'm just curious."

"TJ knows how I feel. He knows I'm not like you…" As I speak the words out loud, I see the empty seat staring back at me. My heart races as I look around to see if I've had an audience watching me yell at an empty space. Fortunately, no one is around, so I just sink in my seat shaking my head. I pull anchor and slowly start the journey home.

After Jen leaves on Sunday afternoon, I sit alone outside on the screened porch of our cabin. My experience from the day before has been weighing heavily on my mind, and the silence is the only thing that keeps my thinking clear.

TJ soon becomes bored. His mother had brought a new energy to us when she came, but now that she's gone, the energy seems to have gone with her. He makes his way onto the porch and sits down in a chair at the table. He can tell that I'm deep in thought and respectfully, he keeps quiet. As my mind comes back to the present, I notice TJ sitting beside me, and I can tell he wants to talk.

"You missing your Mom?"

"Yeah, a lot."

"She's a wonderful lady. I'm a lucky man to have her. Hopefully, you'll meet someone like her and settle down someday."

"That'd be nice. Everything seemed more alive when she was with us," TJ said thoughtfully.

"Did you get to talk with her?"

"About what?"

"Oh, I don't know—anything. I'm just asking. No reason."

"No, we didn't talk about anything new or important."

"Hey! I meant to ask you about those Advanced Placement courses. What do you think about taking them next year?"

"I don't know," TJ said shrugging his shoulders.

"It sounds to me like those courses would be great in helping you prepare for SATs. Maybe you'll get an awesome score and earn an academic scholarship? Hell, that'd be great."

"I don't really want to talk about it."

"Well, why not? You've got the brains to be a great student. Why wouldn't you do well?"

"Look, I don't want to think about college or anything like that. I'm only fifteen years old!"

"Don't get upset."

"I'm not upset!"

"Why do you downplay college like it's this big, bad weight hanging around your neck? Why wouldn't you want to go?"

"Why do you always talk about college and how great it'll be for me? Have you ever considered that maybe I won't go to college or that I might not want to go?"

"No, because you are going to college. Why do you jeopardize your future by not trying your best in school? You have a gift—a gift where learning is easy for you—and you don't care enough to apply yourself. Your teachers say it over and over; yet, you just coast by like you don't give a shit. Your mom and I try to encourage you to see the upside of applying yourself, but you do nothing except sit back and be mediocre."

"Is that what you call it?" TJ countered. "You really believe that what you and Mom do is encouragement? Why don't you try calling it 'smothering,' because that's what it is."

TJ gets more animated as he speaks, and I can tell he's been struggling with this for a long time. He has to get this off his chest, and I think I might have gone too far.

"Son, your education is something that you can't take lightly. I'm sorry if you feel you're being smothered, but I won't apologize for wanting the best for you."

"Well, Dad, I would expect no different. Why would you start to change things now?" TJ said sarcastically. "Why would you listen to me?"

"You just don't get it, and I can't help you understand. You should think about being a doctor, lawyer or a businessman—something that you can do well for yourself and be proud—not an 'everyman' like me. You have the brains to be anything you want to be. You have a gift, and you just need to start using it."

"What's wrong with being an everyman like you?"

"Nothing's wrong with it, but an education will open doors you never thought possible. An education will afford you the opportunity to choose which pathways you want to take in life. It's something that no one will ever be able to take away from you, no matter what happens. I wish I could go back in time and be your age again because I would have pursued a different path. Don't get me wrong—I'm thankful for what I have—but I've also reached a place in my life where my options are few.

"You, on the other hand, have every option right at your fingertips, but you can't see it staring back at you. All you see is that if you can coast through a few more years of school, then you'll be out on your own—making your own way. Sure, it's a great plan for the short term, but then you realize you need to try different things and when you go to open those doors, you find out they're locked. Life turns its back on you, and twenty years later, you look around and ask yourself, *what happened?* And all you can think about is what could have been."

"It sounds like a sad story," TJ said. "But it won't happen to me."

"Okay, Son, whatever you think. Obviously, you have all the answers, and you're not going to listen to me."

"Dad, I'm listening. I just want you to back off and let me do my thing. Stop giving me the gloom and doom story, and let me live my life."

I feel the lump growing in my throat and the swelling in my heart. I had lost my son to my own bad choices. As I listen to TJ, I realize that my words are hollow and empty and that I've lived a mediocre life myself; yet, here I am challenging my son to be better and more successful than I am.

How is he supposed to just listen to my idle conversations when I don't embrace my own bad choices and turn them around? Why is he supposed to treat me any differently than I treated my father, when I act just like him? I'm a fool who's skated by in life for far too long, and this is my consequence.

"TJ, I want you to live your life, your way, but you need to get an education, so you can have options."

"Why?"

"Because it's what's best for you!"

"You didn't, so what gives you the right to tell me what's best for me."

"TJ, don't you see?"

"See what, Dad? See that you're in control? See that you know everything and have all the answers?"

I feel my knees begin to catch and that lump in my throat grows bigger. How can I make him understand? He's fifteen going on forty, and he knows everything. My breathing gets harder and my lungs reach for more air. My chest tightens with every heave, and my heart pounds with a mad fury.

"You just need to see."

"See what? What is it that I need to see?" he screamed.

"You just need to see that I want you to be a better man than my sorry ass—that's all!" I scream back.

At that moment, every emotion I've kept bottled up throughout my life comes pouring out. The tears roll down my face, and I clench my jaw to try and stop the meltdown. My right eye twitches from the stress, and I can't hold it back any longer.

"I'm sorry, TJ, but I've failed you."

I cry harder as I reach for my face and cover my head in shame. My knees weaken and finally buckle under the pressure, and I fall to the ground. As I look up at TJ's face, I can tell he's startled, standing with his mouth half open and his eyes tearing up.

I think about all the time I've missed in his life and all the times we didn't communicate. It bores into my soul like a demonic drill—piercing, stabbing, constricting to every fiber of my being.

"I'm sorry, TJ. I'm so sorry for not being there for you all these years. I'm sorry that we've gotten to this place. I'm just so sorry…"

My body goes limp, and I hang my head again in shame. TJ stands motionless—jaw locked—not knowing what to do and not saying a word. He can't bring himself over to me.

After a few minutes of trying to regain some type of composure, I lift my head and look into TJ's eyes. He's never seen me shed a tear, much less cry uncontrollably. I want to say so much to him, try to explain myself, but nothing comes. As he begins to look away and makes a move to leave, I get enough courage to whisper, "TJ, I love you..."

9 From the moment I broke down, I've thought of nothing more. It's been three weeks since I realized that I'm a failure as a father. TJ is away with his friends—doing God only knows—because he's so bored with me. Everyday, it seems, he disappears for hours at a time, and honestly, most of the time I don't even notice that he's gone.

I sit in this chair on the porch and just stare at the trees and the lake in the distance. I haven't been fishing, or to a fish fry, since everything happened. I can't decide if it's because I just don't feel like it or if I'm too embarrassed to leave the cabin.

Fortunately, TJ is very independent and can take care of himself. He's been doing an excellent job from what I can see. He's stayed to himself a lot, and he's been very respectful of my privacy. I guess he just understands that I need it or something.

My thoughts tend to be harsh at times, and I don't know how to process them. I keep seeing TJ in different stages of his life, and I think about all of the times I've messed up and wasn't there for him. Like when he was three, he loved to play with his trains. He had a train table that we bought him and all of the different shops and stations for the trains to use. When I would come home from work, he would meet me at the door, and I remember the honest, happy look he had for me every night. It was one of the greatest things ever to me.

He would grab my hand and immediately take me to the train table to play. I would sit down and play for about five minutes, complain to him about how tired I was, and then go sit and watch TV until dinner. Afterward, I would go back and park my sorry ass in front of the TV again. For a while, he would try to get me to go back and play, but eventually, he gave up and ended up playing alone.

When I think back on that time, I feel terrible. Those were the years that TJ developed a sense of who he is today and when he formed lasting bonds with those people like his mother he could count on. Sure, I was there for him physically, but I wasn't really there. I was selfish and treated my son with indifference, and I'm ashamed of it.

So many things I've done to him, and I can't begin to know what he's gone through. When he was ten, TJ was really beginning to enjoy playing sports. He took an active interest in the two sports that I love most, football and basketball. It made me proud to know that he wanted to play, and I told him how much I wanted to watch him in action. I even promised that I would help teach him everything I knew about the games. He was so excited, and I was too.

TJ is a physical boy. He always has been. I think he truly enjoyed the physical contact of sports and the competition. Now that I look back, though, I think he started playing sports because I love sports so much, and he wanted to get my attention.

At first, I kept my word, and I made time to watch him play. He was doing so well and excelling in everything. Soon after, I started missing practices, then games, due to work and other things. he played a couple more seasons and then just quit everything all together. At the time, I didn't understand why, but now, it makes perfect sense. What I essentially told him by not showing up was that he wasn't important enough for me to even try to be interested in what he was doing, even though I kept saying all the right things. I was so consumed with myself that I didn't even notice what I was doing to him. Jen tried to tell me in a nice way that I was hurting him, but I just brushed her off like it was no big deal.

No big deal—yeah, that's what I'm proud of at this moment. No big deal that I couldn't put aside a few moments of my night to play trains with my son when he was little. No big deal that I said how important it was for him to play sports and how much I wanted to be a part of it and a part of his life; yet, when the time came to walk the walk, I was nowhere to be found. I guess it should come as no surprise to me now that it's no big deal that my son doesn't want to spend time with me and that I'm the cause of his frustration. Yeah, sure, it's no big deal.

So, here I sit—alone—with nothing but my thoughts. Honestly, I don't like being alone with my thoughts anymore because they keep betraying me. It's tough for someone like me to take. All I think about are my shortcomings and failures. I'm embarrassed by my actions and scared of what the future may or may not bring. I have at least figured out that if I don't change, then I'll end up one day in this same place—alone.

It's funny because my father was so blatant about his feelings, and he alienated my sisters and me by being an ass about everything; yet, in my haste to not be like him, I've ended up doing the same thing to TJ, just in a different way. It makes me mad that I've done similar things and sad that I'm no different.

Last week, I think TJ had enough of my pity party. He came into the cabin and made a beeline to where I was. He stood and looked at me for a moment, then grabbed the closest chair and sat down.

"Dad, I don't know about you, but I'm so bored I can't see straight. When are we going fishing again? I miss it," he said.

I was glad he didn't ask me to relive my finest hour from a couple of weeks ago. He had to know that it was him I couldn't face—no one but him.

"I don't know. Soon, I guess."

"Good, I'll look forward to it," TJ said, and for the first time, I could tell by his body language that he was sincere. "So, what do you think about out here all day?"

Wow! Now there was a loaded question if I'd ever heard one. Strangely, as I looked over at him, he appeared to be genuine as he asked the question—not the malicious teenager trying to prove a point. How do you answer something like that?

Let's see, what could I say that would be appropriate? Oh yes, here it is. Well, Son, I sit and think about everything you've done, and when it came to the most important things in your life and you needed me to be there, I let you down. Now, I'm too ashamed to show my face to you, knowing what you've known for a long time—that I suck as a father.

In the end, I couldn't bring myself to answer the question. "Nothing really. I just sit back and think about this and that."

"Well, okay, just curious."

Of course, I could tell that TJ didn't buy into any of the nonsense I was saying to him, but fortunately, he dropped it.

Every day after that, TJ would come in and spend more time with me, and I felt that for the first time since he was a small child, he really wanted to be with me. His kindness and easy manner made it safe for me to realize that he didn't hate me and that, in some strange way, he actually felt closer to me. I couldn't explain it, and I certainly didn't want to change it because it made me feel good. It also made me want to be a better person and a better father to him.

On Friday, TJ went to the fish fry with his girlfriend Penny, and again, I stayed behind. I took my post on the porch and listened as the frogs and crickets played their songs in the night air. As I sat there, a slow, lone tear rolled down my face as I thought about TJ and all the lost opportunities. I slid out of my chair, crouched down on the hard boards of the deck, and buried my wet face in the pine. I spilled my heart to God.

I prayed for forgiveness, for wisdom, for love, and for understanding. I asked for strength, for courage, and for inspiration to help me be the best father I could possibly be from that day forward. I made a vow to myself and to God that I would be available, honest, and true to TJ and that he would never again know the pain and frustration of having a half-ass parent.

As I stayed on my knees for nearly an hour, pouring out my soul, I had the strangest feeling come over me. It felt like a warm blanket wrapping my cold heart, and my destiny as a father became crystal clear. Where there was once the weight of the world on my shoulders, there was now a tranquil peace of mind—an understanding if you will. Answers to life's questions were revealed to me, and for the first time, my eyes were opened, and I understood the connection between mind, body, and spirit. I knew I'd never be the same, and I knew that I was going to make the most of my life. I didn't know how I was going to do it, but I guessed I would figure that out as I went.

When TJ came in from the fish fry, he made his way to the porch and sat down beside me. We talked about little things, and he was warm and receptive.

"TJ, what do you say about getting up early tomorrow and trying to catch some fish?"

"Dad, I have to say that I would love nothing more," he said, as a smile brushed across his face. "Did I tell you how bored I've been lately?"

As he continued to talk and tell me about all the news from the locals and the funny stories Mike told at the fish fry, I couldn't help but drift off and think about how my life was about to change. I would be a new man—no longer a slave to my father's demons and no longer a man afraid to live, to feel, and to love. I will be the father that my son deserves. The man that I deserve to be.

10 THE LAST FEW DAYS HAVE BEEN REALLY GOOD FOR TJ and me. With my newfound clarity about life, I'm a different person, or so it seems. I believe he can sense the change in me, and he responds in-kind by opening up and talking more. I know it doesn't seem possible in just a few days, but I think we're closer.

On Wednesday, Earl calls and we have a long talk about fishing, fatherhood, and life. He's my best friend, and I'm grateful to have him in my life. Maybe I'm feeling guilty or embarrassed, but I don't come out and share with him all that has happened to me recently. I'm sure he would understand and not judge me because that's what friends do, but it doesn't make it any easier to say.

I do, however, tell Earl about my spiritual awakening, even if I'm a bit vague on the details. Mainly, I want him to know that I've reached a place where I think I understand why Jen sent TJ here with me, and that it's been tough. Earl is receptive and tells me that he's having similar issues with his son, Tim, and he wishes he could find the right things to say and do to make it easier. We've talked about the struggles with our kids many times before, but this is the first time that I believe I might know what to say when the old stuff comes up.

Since Earl told me about this place, I invite him and Tim up for the Fourth of July. A local fishing tournament is scheduled for that weekend. The field will be divided out into groups of four, so all of us could make a formidable team. It will also be a great time to get TJ and Tim together, since they've grown up close and are practically brothers. Earl says he'll think it over and let me know, but he believes he'll come.

At first he's a bit hesitant, but after I tell him about the big Fourth of July festival and fish fry, he starts changing his tune. From what we've learned, the Fourth of July festival is the highlight of the summer. We've been told by all in town that we have to be there, so we plan to be. Besides, I know Earl well enough to know that if he can fish all day and eat and drink all night, then he's as good as here.

As I hang up the phone, another peaceful feeling comes across my soul. Basically, it's the same feeling I've always had when I talk with Earl, but I've never really felt it before. Somehow, my new spiritual sense reaffirms what I've known for years—that Earl is trustworthy, honest and that he would give me the shirt off his back.

Thinking back, I remember the first time I met Earl. I was a couple of months out of the military, and I had just landed a job with the phone company as a technician. Earl was there for his first days as well, and we were placed on the same field team. As the weeks turned into months, he and I became good friends. When we talked, I could tell that he was fond of his privacy, and it took some time before he completely trusted me. We shared our thoughts and ideas on life and happiness, and we even made plans to double date with our wives. Although he was two years younger, he had a solid maturity about him, and I liked that.

At work, Earl was brilliant. He had an aptitude for technology that made the rest of us marvel. For me, learning the new technologies was very difficult at first, and I struggled a great deal. One day when I was near the end of my rope and in jeopardy of losing my job, I went to him for help. He took the time to help and started teaching me what I needed to know. I began to understand what we were learning, and my training started to make sense. Ultimately, I got better and became one of the best linesmen in the company. To this day, I thank Earl for his help in giving me a career to provide for my family.

Outside of work, we started doing more things. Our favorite thing was to go fishing. Although he truly enjoyed it, Earl wasn't a good fisherman at first. Since he had never really had the opportunity to fish growing up, I tried to teach him some things that my father had taught me. I guess it was kind of my way to repay him for all the help he'd given me.

As I kick back on the porch feeling the night air and remembering how Earl and I had become good friends, TJ walks by and sits down.

"You seem to be deep in thought. What are you thinking about?" he asked.

"Well, I just got off the phone with Earl, and I was thinking about the first time we met. Oh, and by the way, I invited him and Tim up for the Fourth of July festival. I think the four of us might do pretty well in the fishing tournament. Somebody's got to beat Mike and the boys."

"Great! I think it's going to be fun. You know, I don't think you ever told me how you and Uncle Earl met."

"Really? I thought I did or he did since he's the big storyteller."

TJ sits there with a smile on his face and shakes his head. "No, neither of you storytellers ever did."

"Okay, well we started two days apart at the phone company something like fifteen years ago."

"No way, you two worked together?"

"Yes, for about two years. I can't believe I haven't told you. We also had our own business, too."

TJ pulls his chair up close and listens intently as I tell him how Earl and I met, how we became good friends, and some funny stories that happened to us over the years. Of all the stories, I think he likes the one about his birth the best, since it shows how completely unprepared we were for his arrival...

"Well, I took your Mom in for her daily check-up with the doctor. It was a Friday, and you weren't due for another two weeks. The doctor had told us that it wouldn't take that long, and she had even guessed that the following Monday would be the lucky day. So, we headed to the appointment thinking we've got the weekend to rest up and prepare, and of course, the doctor says she going to induce labor right away."

"So, what did you do?"

"Well, after picking your Mom up off the floor where she had slowly sunk to her knees, I passed out."

"What!"

"No, just kidding. Just making sure you're listening. We went to the hospital and spent the next six hours trying to get a room. Now, have you ever seen those movies where the pregnant couple leaves the spotless house and grabs the packed suitcase by the door when it's time to go to the hospital?"

"Yes."

"Well, we weren't those people. We thought we had time. I mean you weren't coming until Monday, so why worry? So, we didn't. I spent one minute trying to console your Mom and be there for her, and the next minute trying to reach family members to let them know what was happening. It was chaos, to say the least.

"I finally got Earl on the phone and asked him if he would go over to our house, pack us some clothes, and bring them to us. The funny thing was that he couldn't find anything because the place was a mess, so I had to literally tell him where things were as he walked through the house with the phone in his hand. I don't think he's ever let me forget that."

"That's pretty funny, Dad," TJ said with a smile. "You like Uncle Earl a lot, don't you?"

"Yeah. When it comes to people, there are none better than Earl. He's a great friend, and I can count on him for anything; and him, me."

"I don't think I've ever heard you say that about too many people... maybe Mom, but not even your own family. That's pretty amazing, you know, that you would say that about a friend but not family."

"Well, there really isn't a right way to say it. I guess you need to understand what I mean to understand why I feel the way I do."

I hadn't expected TJ to catch me in a trap, even if he didn't know that he had. Maybe it was my own guilt about my family haunting me and making me uneasy, or maybe I'm over thinking the whole thing. But somehow, I had to explain myself to him.

"TJ, our friends are special people in our lives. Sometimes, they come to us for a short period of time, but they come to us for a reason. Later in life, you'll meet special people who you connect with and come to understand. These people will bring something to your life that you were missing, and it'll help you grow as a person. You may already have friends like this now, and I'm sure that you'll find more as you grow older.

"Friends are great because they're people that you choose to hang around and interact with. They want nothing from you except honesty and truth, and a true friend will not judge you or take advantage of you. He may not like what you're doing or how you're behaving, but he won't piss on you and turn his back on you when things get tight. He might get up in your face when he needs to, and you've got to be ready to do the same for him. But in the end, you have to know that when it's time to go to war, he's got your back. If you know that, and you're lucky enough to find at least one person in your lifetime like that, then you should consider yourself blessed."

"I don't know if I have a friend like that or not...maybe Tim, but he's more like a brother."

"I would say you have one then."

"Yeah, I guess you're right," he replied. "I guess sometimes you just don't know what you have right in front of you."

The words linger in my ears like thunder in the distant sky. TJ has no idea how profound his words are, nor does he have any idea what effect they have on me. I've always tried to pride myself by being 'in the know' on everything, but I notice that I've been missing the obvious right in front of me. The only exception in my life might be Jen, but I can't guarantee that she would agree.

"How right you are. Sometimes, it takes a lifetime to understand it. If we figure it out early in life, then we're lucky. I'm still trying to get lucky."

"I guess you're right," TJ said. "It just seems obvious to me."

Ah, the refreshing purity of youth. I wish I still had his clarity about things. If so, then my life would've gone more smoothly. Why is it when we're young, we look at the glass as half full? Then, as we get older and life kicks us around, we get jaded, stare at the bottom of the glass, and wonder when it will all go away?

Do we end up as pessimists, or are we born that way? It's all a damn shame if you ask me. I guess that's why we look at our children and refer to them as the future. Sure, it's for obvious reasons we do this, but maybe it's even simpler than we know. Maybe, we refer to them as the future because we've given up hope and they haven't yet.

"Dad?" said TJ.

"Yes."

"You said earlier that we choose our friends, but we can't choose our family. What did you mean by that?"

"Nothing bad. It was just an honest answer. We don't get to choose our families and who our parents are—unless you believe in reincarnation or something like that."

"Yeah, but listen to what you're saying. It sounds harsh. It sounds like you're upset that life dealt you a shitty hand, and you got to live with it," TJ said. "How would Grandma feel if she heard you say that—not to mention Aunt Christie or Aunt Cindy?"

Suddenly, my perception of reality comes crashing down around me. How do I answer his question? How do I honestly tell him anything that would remotely make sense? He's not going to believe me anyway, so what's the point?

I don't know the answer. I have to be honest. All my life, I've thought that some things are just simply unfair. Growing up, my friends always had parents who catered to their every need and want while my parents did the best they could for me. All I gained from that experience was an overbearing need to be responsible for everything and everyone around me. That makes it hard for me to truly experience joy and pleasure in my life, and it makes others around me have to carry additional burdens they shouldn't have to.

Maybe I'm pissed that I didn't have the things that others around me had. Maybe I didn't like the fact that my friends all seemed to have these great relationships with their fathers while I got bullshit from mine. I don't know anymore, but I stopped feeling sorry for myself a long time ago. What's the point? Who cares anyway? The only absolute I do know is that I love my mom, my sisters, Jen, and TJ, but the rest is just one big question mark.

"Dad?" TJ said getting my attention.

"Yes."

"How do you think it makes me feel to hear you say those things about your family? You didn't choose me."

Boy, that one hurts. My selfish heart is a clueless bastard sometimes. I lower my head and stare at the ground for a moment, trying to make the emptiness pass, but it doesn't. I couldn't face him, and I have nothing to say—nothing.

Is this how I'm supposed to get the answers from my newfound spiritual sense that I've been bragging about? I'm sitting here like a damn fool with no clever response to avert my son's pointed examination of me. I thought my soul wrenching from before would breathe a refreshing, new life into me; yet, this really sucks. I sit here waiting for the answer, but dark, empty space stares back from my soul instead.

"TJ, I can only imagine how you must feel right now. I can sit here all day and try to make the words make sense, but in all honesty, that's not fair to you. There are times in my life when I look around and think, "Why is this happening to me? What did I do to deserve this?" I can't say that it's right or wrong, but it just is. Sometimes, I feel like I can't take the pressure of being a son, a brother, a husband, and a father, and I want to run away and leave it all behind."

"You do?" TJ asked softly.

"Yes, I do. I'm not proud of it, and I know it makes me sound like a real bastard to you. But anything else I say would be a lie. I sit and think about how life would be so much better if I had been born into a family that actually cared about others—one where we were taught about ourselves and how to survive this world. But I wasn't, and that makes me want to go away and be alone in my own self pity."

TJ slowly rises up out of his chair and begins to leave. As he does, I reach up and gently grab his arm. Our eyes meet, and I can see the confusion in his face. Although he puts up a great front with his clenched jaw and stern look, I can see the fear-stricken child behind the mask, and I don't want him to go away with unfinished thoughts in his head.

"TJ, please wait. Let me finish."

He looks at me with his dark brown eyes, and I can tell instantly that he wants to leave. He starts to make his way to the door but hesitates. I can only imagine what he's thinking right now, and it just kills me to know that I'm the reason, yet again. After a moment passes, TJ makes himself sit back down in the chair.

"Okay."

"TJ, it's true that there are times in my life when the pressure gets so bad, it's almost unbearable. People wanting this and counting on me for that—it just doesn't end. And yes, I do want to run away from it sometimes, but I don't. I don't because I have a wonderful wife that I've loved since the first time I met her, and I have a son that makes me remember why I suck it up and get out of bed each morning. I do it because I love you, and I want you to be proud of me.

"You're right, I didn't choose you, but I'm so blessed you're here. When I have those thoughts of running away, I think of you and your mother together, and I remember that the two of you represent the only peace I have in my life. I have only a few absolutes in this world, and the most important one is that I love you both dearly."

The fear subsides from TJ's face as he looks back at me. We don't speak for a long time after that because we each understand that nothing more needs to be said. I had come clean with him as honestly as I could, and although it wasn't easy, I think it helped us both take a small piece of the other away from that moment.

11 SOMETIMES, I DON'T KNOW WHAT TO THINK ABOUT life. Just as I think I have something figured out, I realize that I know nothing. How am I supposed to teach any sort of wisdom to another person when I have no clue as to what wisdom really is? Is it something that's bestowed upon us, or is it something we learn over time?

It's just like the other day. I thought I was on to something—having a newfound spiritual sense. I thought that my enlightenment would come, and I would be able to quote Shakespeare, understand the theories of Jung, and decode the mysteries behind the works of Da Vinci, or something like that. Hell, I was really just hoping to understand a little of what TJ was thinking. Instead, I got nothing but confusion, and my attempt to be spiritually enlightened didn't go the way I planned. I wanted to help TJ, but I ended up examining the darker parts of myself.

Jen constantly tells me that if I ever want to understand and reach a higher plane, then I need to surrender to it. That all sounds really good in theory, but what the hell is it that I'm surrendering to? And what does that mean? I thought I surrendered when I broke down and dumped my soul to God. But here I am, weeks later, and I feel the same. Sure, I'm a little more raw inside, but I don't feel as great as I did those first few days after that eventful night. So does this mean that spirituality is only temporary or a fictitious ideal we try to obtain? I just don't know.

The summer rain sounds so good to me this evening. This porch has become my temple, my sanctuary from the world. I sit here, and I listen to the rain, the wind, and the sounds of darkness. I think about my life, and I have to say, I don't like it. I just wish I knew why I can't seem to grasp the spiritual plateau that so many speak of because right now, I think I can use a little of it.

Ah, the breeze is nice. There's nothing like a summer breeze cooling the night air after a good, soaking rain. The rain came so rapidly that I can still smell it in the night. It's refreshing, even purifying in a way. TJ went to bed about an hour ago, and like many nights these past few weeks, I'm staying up to reflect on the day.

As the time passes, I feel my eyes getting heavier and heavier. The peacefulness of the night makes it easy for me to drift into a semi-conscious place. I sit back, relax in my chair and listen for all of the dreamy sounds of summer.

"Wake up!" said a quiet voice from the chair across the room.

"What?" I say as I startle myself. "Who is it?"

"Oh, come on Tom, do we really have to do this same dance again?" he said. "Always with the disbelief."

"Great. Can't you just leave me alone?" I know in an instant that my father has stopped by to pay me a visit. Maybe my karma is showing itself since I said he had his demons to work out. Now, apparently, I have my own demon, and he's haunting me after his death.

"Tom, Tom, Tom. The bitterness in your voice disappoints me—I have to tell you. Why can't you just give me a break? I am dead, you know," he said, baiting me into confrontation.

"Why don't you just leave me alone? I know you aren't real and that I'm dreaming. As soon as I wake up, you won't be here."

"Well, honestly, Son, I like coming to visit you. It more or less makes my day."

I know what he means without thinking about it. You can't live with someone for years and not know the hidden meanings in the words he says. He enjoys torturing me—just like he did when he was alive.

"You're still an asshole. I hope you know that."

"Well, now, why would I think you would think any differently of me now that I'm dead? You can't hurt me anymore, so think what you want about me. I don't care."

"What do you mean, I can't hurt you anymore? You're the one that's hurt me my whole life."

"What's there to say, Tom? You hurt me so much with your smug attitude and the fact that you think you know everything," he said. "You've never listened to anything I've said."

"What? Are you serious? I did everything to try to please you, but you never cared enough to see it. I did anything to just get your attention for a moment, but I got nothing but crap from you."

"What about you and your controlling nature? Everything always had to be done Tom's way, or there was hell to pay for the rest of us. Yeah, I said it. And what about the fact that everything I did was for you and your sisters? You are an unappreciative, controlling bastard. You've been that way since you were born, and as you've gotten older, it's only gotten worse. I had to be hard on you because if I weren't, you would've swallowed us all up with your negativity."

"How dare you say that about me! I loved you, and I wanted to be you when I grew up. But the older I got, the more I realized I wanted to be nothing like you because you were a rude and bitter person whose selfishness drove everybody away."

My blood begins to boil, and I'm prepared to stay out here and go toe-to-toe with this son-of-a-bitch all night if I have to. I know what happened, and I'm not letting him get away with these lies. I was tired of his bullshit growing up, and I'm tired of it now, too. This fight ends tonight because I'm over it.

"You got anything to say?"

"Yes, I do. You're a damn fool."

"What? You son of a bit…" I yell as I stand up from my chair, ready to cross the room and finish the argument. I hesitate and slowly sit back down.

His voice is cracking with emotion as he speaks. "Actually, we're both damn fools. We've been playing this silly game for years, and we've nothing to show for it. Now I'm gone, and we can never get back the lost time. All the arguments, all the pain, and now, we have nothing but deep-rooted anger toward each other. When will it end?"

"I don't know."

"You can try to deny it however long you want, but you're just like me. You're making the same mistakes I did. The longer you hold onto it, the more the anger will eat at you and destroy the relationships with the ones you love the most," he said. "Tom, all we have is today, and yesterday is gone."

I feel my anger leave and my heart pound with a deep sadness. I drop my head into my hands and cover my eyes. I'm trying hard to hold my composure and to think about his words. Still looking down, I speak as honestly as I can. "I'm sorry for the pain I caused you. I know it may be a little late, but Dad, I love you."

There is no answer coming from him, and I know he's gone. A large tear begins to roll down my face, and although I can't bring myself to let go, I take the moment for what it is and remember my father for everything he was—good and bad.

All of the struggles, the arguments, and the anger—I remember them all. Strangely, I also begin feeling the strength and the love he brought. I think I've pushed it so far down that I've forgotten it even existed. Maybe his way isn't what I think is best, but it was his way. He did try.

I also remember the way I handled myself, the things I said, and the pain I caused. We were two headstrong people constantly in battle, neither willing to give anything to the other. Now, as I sit here, all I have are these memories that I can't change—memories that show how much effort was spent on things that aren't worth it, things that I can never take back, and things I'll regret for the rest of my life.

All we have is today, and yesterday is gone. Those words will haunt me for the rest of my life, not only because they speak the truth about my relationship with my own father but also because they represent fifteen years of lost time with TJ. I've spent my time searching for the answer to have peace and joy in my life, and when I finally learn it, it's my father who teaches me. Imagine the irony in that.

He's right. We are all damn fools if we don't believe that we have only a short time to be around those we love. If we don't make the most of it, we end up sitting on a porch in the early morning hours having heated conversations with an empty chair trying to figure it all out.

I hear the backdoor creak, and I quickly turn around to see TJ making his way outside. "Dad," he said softly.

"Yes."

"Are you okay?" he asked. "I heard voices out here, and I thought I'd come out and check on you."

"Yeah, Son, I'm fine," as I catch myself with an embarrassed grin on my face. "There's nobody out here but me. I've resorted to talking to myself, it seems."

"Are you answering yourself?" TJ asked trying to break the heaviness of the mood.

"Well, since you ask, I must confess that I am. Unfortunately, not all the answers are good and what I want to hear."

TJ's eyes get a little wider than normal as he listens to me. His facial expressions clearly show that he wasn't expecting me to say that, and he looks like he's searching for something to say.

"Okay, I was only kidding, but it's cool…maybe a little more information than I needed, but it's good."

Releasing the emotion, I begin laughing. Soon, he starts laughing, too, and I can't help but think how crazy I must seem to him right now. It's as if all of his curiosities about my mental health have been confirmed. So, I laugh some more.

The thing is I'm noticing that life is funny when we deal with the absurdities we bring on and create for ourselves. But it's good to look across the chair at my flesh and blood and know that I've still got time to share moments like this with him—crazy or not.

"Dad, sometimes I just don't know about you."

"Well, I don't really know about me either. Aren't you lucky you've got me to look up to? Aren't you excited to see what you're going to become?" At this, we both start laughing again. I'm laughing so hard that my sides are aching and my eyes are watering.

"I figured something out tonight, and it's so simple. I can't believe that I never got it before."

"What did you figure out?"

"I figured out what it is. I figured out the secret of *wa*."

"What? What in the world is *wa*?"

"It's a word I read about a long time ago. It's a Japanese word which means peace and harmony—something I've been seeking my whole life. Now, I know the secret."

"Well, what is it?"

"I don't know if I should tell you or not. Maybe I should let you figure it out for yourself. It's taken me years to understand. I've had people like your mother trying to guide me, but now, it's crystal clear."

"Dad, just tell me."

"We all spend our lives in a constant battle for knowledge and control, and we seek peace as a refuge from ourselves. Our spirituality is based on what we learn and comprehend from these moments of complete tranquility that we find ourselves. The problem is that society puts pressure on us to constantly go here and go there, do this and do that, and we never stop to take time for ourselves. We never take a step back from life to examine ourselves from within."

"Is that the secret of *wa*?"

"Not entirely. The secret to achieving *wa* is surrender—surrender of your life and the control we all try to have."

I can hear Jen in my head, standing behind me saying, *"What have I been saying all these years? Some revelation—I told you this ten years ago."* Then, she would come over, kiss me on the cheek, and get one last parting shot. *"Since I know you actually do listen, I'll start making my list for the next ten years."* Her half-grin would flash, and she would move onto other things, confident that she knew it all along.

"Dad, Mom says that surrender stuff all the time. It's no big deal."

"True. She does say that we should surrender our lives to become more spiritual." I look quickly over my left shoulder—then the right—to make sure that the coast is clear. "And she's right!" I jump back in my seat, double-checking every corner of the porch to make sure Jen hasn't secretly arrived and is hiding in the shadows waiting for the exact moment I acknowledge her brilliance. I truly expect a big 'A-ha!' from behind the chair and an omnipotent finger pointing in my face, followed by several "I told you so's."

TJ looks at me like I am crazy, but I'm completely unaffected by it since we'd already established that a little while ago. Still, he just shakes his head in disbelief.

"But the part I've been searching for is just as simple. See, when we surrender our lives to God, we experience the peace and harmony of *wa*; however, it's always short-lived because when we get to that spiritual place, we quickly lose sight of it, starting to believe that we have all the answers. Our ego gets in the way, and our *wa* is gone. The secret is to surrender to it again and again to maintain it, realizing that once we get there, our spiritual journey is only beginning, not ending."

"I don't think I understand," TJ said sounding a little frustrated.

"I don't expect you to."

"What does that mean?"

"It means nothing. I don't expect you to fully understand it right now because you haven't experienced the ups and downs of life. You will soon enough, and believe me, there's no reason to rush it. I just want you to be aware that *wa* exists, and when you realize that it's what you're seeking, you will know what to do."

"But how will I know what to do? How will I know when I see it?"

"You will know when you choose to see it. It's always right there in front of you—in front of us all. We just don't take the time to recognize it and make the choice to surrender to it."

"How can I choose it if it's right in front of me? Isn't the choice already made at that point?"

I love innocence. It's such a breath of fresh air to be around. I literally love to hear the words come out of his mouth. I remember a time not too long ago when I was idealistic and questioned everyone and everything. But as time went by, I lost my yearning for the answers and got stuck in the rut of life, longing for the tranquility of the moment.

Maybe it's because life bitch-slaps us around a little too much, and in our punch-drunk state, we give up. Maybe that's just how it is except for the few lucky ones who figure it out. Maybe we've all got shit, but it's dressed up all pretty and we get fooled. But like everyone really knows; underneath, it's all still shit. Maybe it is—I don't know—but unless I change it, how will I ever know if there's something better out there?

"TJ, your questions are valid, but before I go too far and we end up in an argument, I'm going to stop and let you figure it out. Once you do, you'll understand."

"When will I understand?" TJ asked, wanting the answer. To me, this is a prime example of the 'me-now' generation, always wanting the solution and not waiting for the answer.

"You will know when. You will grow older and wiser as the years go by, and you, like all of us, will search for the understanding—the spiritual harmony—to life. This will be the first part of your spiritual journey, and there's no timetable for it to come—it just will. I can say this to you now because I'm living it tonight. I've been searching for a long time, but now, I'm crystal clear. I realize that there's so much more for me to learn."

"But how long do I wait?" TJ asked. "I just want to know when."

"TJ, don't worry about when because if you do, you'll never surrender and find the answer. You just need to have the courage to make it happen, and it will. We've sat and talked these past couple of months about religion and many other things. Now is the time to use what you know of God and have faith that everything's going to be okay."

"Okay...I hope you're right."

"I believe that I am. In the future, when you're at your wit's end and you're searching for something—anything—to make sense, just remember this conversation."

12 A COUPLE OF DAYS LATER, TJ AND I DECIDE TO GET up early and hit our favorite spots before the sun comes up. We've done this about four or five times since we arrived, and we've had good success. Mike had told us this was a good technique to use when the hot weather started coming in, and we figured that by trying it a few times, we would be ready when the really hot weather came.

The logic made sense to me, especially since most fish go deeper to cooler water in the hot summer. By getting out before the sun came up, we were able to fish like we had in the spring. Although a little unnerving at first because of the limited sight distance and other added dangers of being on such a big lake in the dark, we quickly found that getting out early makes for a new adventure every time.

The only problem with leaving so early is that by ten o'clock, we're both exhausted. Instead of going back to the cabin and then coming back out later, TJ and I come up with the idea to take turns napping on the boat while the other one fishes. It's actually a pretty good idea because we're both able to sleep, but more importantly, it gives each of us the opportunity to fish alone peacefully.

I usually let TJ sleep first, and I take advantage of the peace every chance I get. Today, for some reason, I'm not very tired as the morning lull hits. TJ, of course, is out like a light on his side of the boat, and the sun is beating down on us from above. The fish had stopped biting, as they do everyday when it gets hot, and I take a moment to reflect on all that has happened.

I can't help but chuckle softly when I think about my original mission in coming here. My goal had been to be alone and resolve some issues I had with my father—none of which have come to pass. Then, Jen drops a bomb and sends TJ with me for the whole trip. I remember feeling angry with her at first for sending him, and then something inside me told me that selfishness would only go so far. Plus, I thought the trip might be a golden opportunity for me to straighten him out a little and let him know who's the boss. I knew that if he listened to me, he might learn something he could use later in life.

Now, after two breakdowns, conversations with a ghost, and the sheer embarrassment at times of not being able to look my son in the face, I can honestly say—mission accomplished—no sanity issues here.

Later, after TJ awakes, we find an island shade to cover us as we stop to eat lunch. The day, like so many others, is nasty from the heat and added humidity. Oddly enough, TJ doesn't complain about the heat like he usually does, so for me, the day is already better. I honestly never hold it against him when he complains because being tired and cranky runs in the family, and any lack of sleep only worsens the matter.

We had agreed the night before that we were going to stay out all day and see if it made any difference in how many fish we caught. Our days usually end around two o'clock. Today at three-thirty, there is no visible difference in our catch, yet we're determined to make it the whole day.

My hours of sleeplessness finally catch up with me, and I have to stop for a short nap. I clear out a spot on my end of the boat and lay my head back on the edge. The sun is still warm, but the intensity of the heat has finally let up. As I lay back, I feel the sun's rays warm my face, and I listen as the waves smack the nearby buoys—clang, clang—sounding as if a bell has tolled in the distance. The sound isn't loud; rather, just enough to let you know they're there. The boat rocks slowly as the small swells hit against the sides. My mind slowly begins to drift, and the sleep starts to overtake my body. As it always did, the calm of the lake has filled my spirit with peace, and my *wa* is good.

This time, there is no voice coming from the other side, and I have no feelings of anger, resentment, or remorse about my father. Even the overall loss is somehow easier to take. Perhaps I've finally let it go, surrendered to it, and made peace with my demon? Maybe I've grown up a little in the process and have become a better man? Regardless, I'll definitely be different.

As I awake, I can feel the cool rays of the sun on my face, and I know that dusk is approaching. I stand up and slide back into my chair, glancing over at TJ. He seems to have enjoyed his time alone and looks tired but content. I give him a quick grin and turn my sights to the setting sun. After spending these last few months with me, TJ knows that silence is best for me during this time. I only want nature and the tranquility she brings with her.

I can't help but think of all the times I've escaped to the lake to watch the sunset, just trying to find a peaceful moment in the day to escape the wrath of my father. The irony now is that when I look back at our many fishing trips together, I realize that he, too, loved the sunset on the lake at dusk. It's the only time I ever saw him relax and take a step back from life. I escaped from him to find peace and ended up finding peace the same way he did. Maybe he did teach me something after all?

"TJ?"

"Yeah."

"Do you think any of us have joy in our lives?"

"I don't know. Do you?"

"Honestly, I don't know either."

"How would you know? How would anyone know?"

"That's a good question. I'm sitting here thinking about all of the times I've felt the warm rays of the sun on my face and experienced the peace that comes watching the sunset on the lake, but I don't know if I've ever felt joy with it. I've said many times that I believe we're all searching for peace and harmony in our lives. I still think that's true, but if we don't experience joy, then are we missing something?"

"But haven't you experienced joy in some things during your life?"

"Well, yes of course. I've experienced joy when you were born and when your mother said, "Yes," when I asked her to marry me. I guess I'm talking more about life in general—the big picture—the little things we face everyday that gets us down.

"I feel as though I've spent my entire life trying to control everyone and everything. My family and friends just let it go because it's me and how I am, but that's not right. All I've done in trying to control everything is create fear, anxiety, and stress in my life, and I've made those around me pay for my shortcomings. It's also tainted my view of the beauty in life, and now I want peace, love, and joy instead. Does that make sense?"

"Yep, it does. It seems to me that if you want peace, love, and joy in your life, then you must choose to make it happen—wouldn't you say?" TJ asked with a pretentious grin.

"So, I guess you do listen after all?"

"Sometimes," he replied. "I would think that as soon as you make peace with yourself and your issues, then joy comes. That's what makes sense to me."

"I think you're pretty smart. Obviously, you did get some things from me."

"Thanks," TJ said, as he slyly glances my way and grins. It's easy to tell when our eyes meet that we both know the real truth about where his smarts come from, but hey, it's fun to pretend.

I sit amazed at the innocent clarity in his thoughts. His reasoning is quick, and it makes perfect sense. Other than the basic fact that he's right, I just feel my body flowing with pride when I look at him and listen to what he's saying. It's tough because it's like he's got a magical daddy cue card, and all my flaws are listed for him to exploit. Every time he hits home with me, I hate it and love it at the same time.

"Dad," said TJ.

"Yes."

"How do you think Grandma's doing?"

"Fine, I guess. You miss her?"

"Yes, a lot."

TJ had spent a lot of time with his grandmother in the last year. They had developed an even stronger bond than they had when he was younger. I don't know if it's just an inherent thing that grandparents and children get along so well, but it always seems to be the case.

Maybe grandparents have lived long enough to know what works and what doesn't with kids? Maybe they figure it's time to see if they would've been more successful if they had done things differently? Or maybe, once you reach a certain age, you revert back to childhood, and you're on the kids' level, so they understand you? Regardless of what it is, it works.

My Mom and TJ share many things, and it's obvious they're so much alike. Looking at them both and their approach to life, it tells me that I still have lessons to learn in my life—lessons I didn't learn growing up. I've always been so serious about life, and both my Mom and my son are outgoing, fun-loving people. I think my challenge is to teach them both how to take life more seriously and be responsible, and I think they're here to help me loosen up and enjoy life more.

My Mom has always been my rock. She was the only one who held the family together when we were young. She understood that my father was difficult to deal with—probably more than anyone—and she tried her best to make it all okay. She taught me the value of people and the need to be honest with myself and those around me. She gave me the foundation for courage to be an independent person and thinker and to make good decisions.

Even though she still doesn't completely understand me, and we disagree on a variety of issues—even to the point where my frustration level gets so high—I love her. I love her for who she is, and I'm grateful for her sacrifice to make me a better person. She's the only one who's been there for me my entire life, and I take true comfort in that.

I feel bad now because I know she feels alone since my father died, and I really haven't been there for her. Looking back, I guess I had to get things right with myself first before I could do her any good. I hope she understands, and I think she will. When we get back, I need to make it a priority to show her I'm here for her. I need to do that for me and for her.

"Me, too. Let's call her when we get back to the cabin tonight. Sound good?"

"It does! Yes, it does!"

13 It's hard to believe we've been here a few months. I can't say that we've actually had fun, but the time has flown by. Well, okay, so some of the time has been fun. It's by far a heck of a lot more fun now than it was.

I still enjoy the Friday night fish fries the best, especially after missing several of them last month. The people are so friendly, and no one ever questioned why I didn't come and sent TJ alone. Of course, he went with his girlfriend, so I doubt anybody thought much of it. In fact, when I came back, I was treated like I had never left, and I knew things were okay when Alice Higgins pulled me aside.

"I've baked another peach pie, and I know you love them. I was hoping you would be here tonight because I saved you an extra slice to take back home," she said. "I just had to, since you made over it so much last time."

"Well, thank you. I feel special now because I know there will be many people trying to get their hands on a slice. I appreciate your kindness, and I won't tell anybody."

"Good. I'll see you before I leave," she whispered.

Alice Higgins is a spirited, white-haired lady of about sixty-five. She is the town's grandmother, and no one can match her cooking. For a woman, who stands all of five feet, she has the biggest heart and the brightest smile of anyone we've met since we've been here.

Her husband, Dave, is a sweet and kind man. He's someone you can listen to all night because he tells such great stories. He actually reminds me a lot of how Earl will be at that age. You can tell that when he speaks of Alice, he knows he hit the lottery and he's a lucky man. Forty-five years of marriage, and they're still going strong—not to mention they're still talking.

I hope when I get to his age, I can look over at Jen and have that same look on my face that Dave does when he looks at Alice. What a true love they must have, and I think anyone who looks at them has to be a little jealous.

About three weeks after we arrived, TJ and I were driving along trying to figure out different places in town. We came upon a car pulled to the side of the road, and we stopped to make sure everything was okay. When we approached the car, we saw stark-white hair and big blue eyes staring back at us. We didn't know her at the time, but Alice rolled down her window and smiled at us with the warmest, friendliest smile I'd ever seen. I was surprised to say the least because we were two strangers in her small town, and where we're from, people tend to think the worst. Alice didn't care.

"Well, hello there," Alice said. "I'm Alice Higgins, and you?"

"Hello, I'm Tom Phillips, and this is my son, TJ. Are you alright?"

"Oh yes, I'm fine," she answered. "I'm afraid I have a flat tire, and I've got deliveries to make."

"We'll be glad to help you. Just pop open the trunk and let me see if you've got everything you need."

"Oh, thank you."

After thirty minutes, we were finally finished changing the tire, and we were soaking wet with sweat and plastered with grease up to our elbows.

"All done."

"Here, let me pay you for helping me. I don't know what I would've done if you hadn't come along."

"Sorry, but we can't accept your money. We're just glad we were driving around and able to help."

"Well, if you won't accept money, then please take a fresh, homemade apple pie with you. I baked it this morning," she said, as she grabbed the pie out of the backseat.

"Well, don't twist my arm too hard. I guess I must be too easy because I heard the words homemade and pie, and my defenses crumbled."

"Don't worry about it, honey—it happens all the time," Alice said, as she winked at TJ. "I have to say, if I knew I was going to be rescued by two handsome young men, then I might have to have a flat tire more often."

With that, Alice hopped back into her car, rolled down her window and said, "I'm sure I'll see you again. Why don't you come to the fish fry on Friday night? It's going to be lots of fun."

"We'll try," TJ said before I could say anything. He obviously liked Alice very much. Honestly, who could blame him, as I was pretty sure the whole town did, too.

Ever since that fish fry, Alice has saved a slice of pie for me to take back home. She even sent slices home with TJ, when I didn't go. She's a great lady and a wonderful cook. She's slowly becoming my new best friend.

I found out a short time later that Alice and Dave own a bakery in town, and she was known from far away as having the best desserts in the state. Yet another example of the true kindred spirit that we both share. Actually, TJ and I volunteered to make deliveries for her, so she and Dave could spend time together. She was still working, but according to others in town, she didn't have to. She kept working because she loved it, and she loved giving to others.

The more I talked with Alice, and the more I talked with others about her, I became more and more intrigued with her. She made me think about my life and my work in a different way, and the thought of doing something because you love it was just a strange concept to me. I've always believed that you go to work to make money, have stuff, and pay the bills. You don't go because you want to, but because you have to.

Now, here was this lady who had money, a great husband, good friends and a giving soul—somebody who could've retired years ago— yet she did everything because she wanted to do for others and give. I've thought about it from the first time I found out about her, and I continue to think about it everyday since because I've just never met anyone like her.

Later that weekend, TJ and I are talking and he asks me a question. I don't know what he wants to find out, but I think I will run with it and see where we end up.

"Dad," said TJ.

"Yes."

"Why does Ms. Alice always send us home with a slice of pie?"

"She's just being nice."

"She is nice. But don't you think that she's more than paid us back for helping her?" he asked. "I mean, how much extra pie can she give us?"

"Hold on. Did you say—give us?"

"Uh," TJ mumbled. He's caught and he knows there's no denying it. I know he has to come clean when a big smile comes across his face, and I think he even blushes.

"Well, Dad, it's like this," he said in mock defense. "Ms. Alice might sneak me an extra slice of pie during the fish fry, but I'm not completely sure."

"I see, holding out on me—I can't believe it. And here I thought I was the special one. Ms. Alice is quite slick."

"Dad, by now, I'd think you would know better," TJ said with a grin. "Besides, you never answered my question."

"Well, I don't think it's about the pies or necessarily paying us back for helping her. She's obviously done more for us than we have for her. I just think she has a giving spirit and a warm heart."

"She is giving and she really seems to enjoy herself."

"Yes, she does! And I am so envious!"

"Dad."

"Yeah."

"Do you enjoy what you do?" he asked. "Are you happy with your job?"

Happy? How do you determine if you're happy—especially with work? TJ has a way of finding my open wounds when my defenses are down. There are so many things he doesn't understand yet like how a simple question of happiness creates such a complicated answer. Am I happy? I don't know for sure. I'm sure as hell not as happy as Ms. Alice is. Actually, compared to her, I'm a miserable bastard.

"Am I happy with my job? Now, there's a loaded question."

"Why?"

"Because one day you'll be in it, and then you'll get asked an easy question like that, and you'll be searching for an answer."

"But that makes no sense."

"Exactly. Welcome to another lesson on real life."

"That's the easy way out."

"You may be right. I'll answer your question. The fact is that I don't know if I'm happy or not with my job. I thought I was, but then we came here and met Ms. Alice. I've watched her closely and realized that she genuinely loves what she does, and she gives to others from her heart. To me, she's the one that's happy—happy with her job, happy with herself, and happy with life. Looking at myself, what I thought was happiness is only shades of contentment. Some might even call it comfort in complacency, and if it's truly the case, then no, I'm not happy."

"Dad, I don't mean to be critical, but you've got a lot of problems," TJ said, as he flashes a quick grin my way.

Of course, some of the most truthful things are said in jest. "Don't hold back on my account son. Let me know what you really think about me."

"I don't mean it like that. It's just that I never see you smile, and you hardly ever just goof-off and do something out of the ordinary," said TJ. "You're only thirty-six years old, and you still have so much ahead of you. What's gotten you like this?"

Two steps forward, one step back. Just when I think I'm making progress and trying to get off the ground to stand on my own two feet, I'm knocked down again. It's just so hard to stay focused when everything seems to come crashing down around you. I just want something to go my way. Something—anything—please!

"I don't know. Bad choices, I guess."

"What bad choices?"

"When I think about my job and where I'm at in life, I start to feel inadequate, and it makes me mad that I chose security over happiness."

"What do you mean?" asked TJ. "I don't understand what you mean about security over happiness."

"When you were four years old, I was laid off from my job at the phone company. It was completely unexpected, and I was devastated and had no idea what we were going to do to survive."

"I didn't know that."

"There was never any reason to tell you, and of course, you wouldn't have understood it at four. You just asked me why I wasn't going to work, but other than that, you didn't know the difference."

"How long were you without a job?"

"Three months. Probably the hardest three months of my life."

"What did you and Mom do to get by? Was it really hard?"

"I probably never mentioned it before because things got better, and I got another job that was similar to my old job. After that, I settled in, worked, got my paycheck and turned a blind eye to my feelings about what happened; however, I've never been able to turn off the resentment that's followed and been with me all these years. It's hard because you think you're supposed to have some type of loyalty from your company, especially since you go in everyday and bust your ass to do a great job, but what you find out is that you're just headcount—an empty chair filling up space."

"I always thought you loved working for the phone company. That's all I hear you and Mom talking about at night."

"No, I certainly don't love the phone company. I chose the safe and secure route—the same path I've taken all my life. I was afraid to get out and see what the world had to offer. I was afraid to better myself and get out of my comfort zone. I still am."

Looking at TJ, I can tell he doesn't quite understand what I mean. How can I expect him to? He's only fifteen, and I remember at fifteen, I had no clue either.

"It's not fun, is it?"

"What's not fun?"

"Real life in all its glory." As I speak the words, I can see TJ retreating and thinking to himself. We go for awhile before either of us speaks again.

I finally have to say something because I basically tainted his optimistic view of life yet again. Sure, I'm exaggerating, but it has to have an effect on him when his father does nothing but give him negativity in his life.

"TJ."

"Yes."

"I'm sorry."

"It's okay, Dad," he said. "It's really okay."

"Actually, it's not. I have no right to dump my anger and frustration, for my bad choices, on you."

"I know you didn't mean it."

"Well, the sad part is that I do mean it, but I've got to own up to the fact that I'm responsible for my actions. No one else forced me to make the decisions I've made—no one, but me."

I stop for a moment and listen to my own words as they fade into the silence. If I were in therapy, I'm positive my therapist would tell me that this is a crowning moment in my recovery. Funny, honesty has always been the thing I've lived by, and I've been honest with everyone but myself. It's damn hard to listen to yourself and be critical.

"TJ, a man is defined by what he does for a living. A lot of people think that this is an absurd way to value a person's worth, and it may be. But think about this for a moment—after you're introduced to someone, what's the first question asked? I'll tell you—it's what do you do?"

"I don't hear too much of that right now, but again, I'm only fifteen," TJ said with a smile.

"Very funny, but trust me, you will. Remember this, there's nothing wrong, and everything right about getting an honest day's pay for an honest day's work. That, in itself, is the basic principal that separates people. You can't lie or cheat your way around it, because it'll always find you out.

"I also believe that you should take my advice and learn to use your head, not your back like I do. You'll do better for yourself in the end. You make it a point to work smarter, not harder, and you must find a job that you love to do—one that makes you want to give to others through service and leadership. I tell you this as someone who didn't do it this way—someone who sits on the wrong side of bad decisions. Someone who wants only the best for you as you go through life."

"I think I understand."

"Good, because you have what it takes to make a difference, and if you learn it now, it'll stay with you forever."

"I'll try my best."

"Thanks."

It's an odd thing for me to say thanks to TJ because I've always approached our relationship with the belief that he should just listen to me because I'm his father. Now, I realize that being a father is one thing and earning my son's respect is another. Lesson learned, I hope.

"Dad."

"Yes."

"You said a couple of things earlier that I don't get."

"Okay, what are they?"

"Well, the first one deals with how a man is defined," he said. "How can someone be defined by what he does for a living? That makes no sense to me. Do you believe that?"

"I did up until about a month ago. Hell, I've lived the lie."

"But I don't get why it's like that. And why would you suddenly change now?"

"Because your dad learned something from a little, old lady."

"Ms. Alice?"

"Yep, Ms. Alice. Up until we came here, I believed like all those others that you are what you do. I played the game, asked the same questions and tried to see where I stacked up in the mix of things. I'm just as shallow as everyone else."

"So, what did you learn, and how did Ms. Alice help?"

"After we first met Ms. Alice, I became curious as to whether or not she was the real deal. I started asking around, and every person I spoke with told me the same thing about her—that she was just a great lady. So, I made it my mission to try and figure out what her secret was, and now I know. Ms. Alice is all about giving and doing for others—no strings attached. She genuinely cares about others, and she helps them from her heart. She does it in all aspects of her life and that makes her special. She can't be defined by how many pies she's baked, or how much money she's made. She's defined by how many lives she's touched and how much good is brought from it. She's taught me to look at people in a different way and to not judge them, or have them judge me, based on a silly accepted social practice. Who cares what we do for a living? It's what we do the rest of the time the we should be concerned about."

"Does it make you want to change your life?"

"You bet it does."

"Well, that kind of leads me to my second question."

"How so?"

"You said earlier that you were laid off from the phone company for three months, and that you chose security and went back to work for them when they offered you another job, right?"

"Yeah, so what's your point?"

"My question is this—have you ever stopped long enough to figure out what makes you happy?" TJ asked. "Would you still be working at the same company? I'm just curious."

Who needs to pay for therapy? Just take your teenager on a summer trip and talk about things. Since he knows all your flaws, he'll be able to easily ask the questions you've been avoiding. Hell, I may just loan him out to my friends for a small fee.

Happy? What would make me happy? To stop answering deep questions about my life and my feelings—now, that'd make me happy. It's just like everything else, it's not easy to answer or think about right now.

"I don't know, TJ. There are some things I thought I would try and might like, but I don't know."

"There has to be something."

"TJ, when you get to be a dad, you just settle in and go with the flow. You look at things more responsibly and ask yourself what's more important—education, more money, or a healthy 401K and benefits package? You put thoughts of what you could've done on the back-burner, and you look for things you can get lost in to manage the stress and gain a moment of peace."

"That's a bullshit answer, Dad," TJ said emphatically. "What happened to all the talk about how 'You can be anything you want to be,' or 'Use your brain, not your back'?"

"That was for you."

"If it's good enough for me, then why isn't it good enough for you? You're freaking thirty-six years old, not on your last go-around. Why should I listen to you and try to do and be all these things, when you won't?"

Got me! No comeback to my own words. No clever one-liners to mask the moment.

"Surely, there's something you would like to do," TJ said, as his patience wears thin.

"Fine. I've always thought about going back to school and getting my college degree. I believe in it so much, and I'd like to do it. I'd also like to start buying real estate and turning it into investment opportunities. I have the skills to be a good carpenter, and I think I'd like to see if I have the smarts to do it right. Mostly, I just want to be free from corporate America and its bullshit. I just want to choose my spot in the world and dictate things on my terms when life tries to kick me around. I want to wake up in the morning and know that I love who I am. Whatever I do, I want to know that I'm serving and leading others."

It feels good to speak aloud about what I want and what I would like to do. In fact, it's exciting and liberating. I've never told anyone of my desires before, not even Jen. For some reason, I feel she might think I'm not qualified or something. In all honesty, I'm afraid of what she might think of me, especially if I fail. In reality, I know she would be supportive and giving, just like she is all of the time.

"Dad."

"Yeah."

"If you want those things, then why don't you do them? Don't think about why you can't. Think about what it'll take to make them happen," TJ said with the wisdom of Solomon.

I hesitate before I answer. Always one to think first, I never give my word unless I intend to follow through. So much to grasp. So much to take in. So much to be proud of. So much change. Finally, broken and knowing he's right, "Okay, I will if you will."

"Deal."

14

TJ AND I ARE ALWAYS OUT ON THE BOAT FISHING AND doing our same routine—fishing early, fishing late and a little fishing in between. We're regulars in town, and we're enjoying our stay as much as possible, even though we both are a little homesick.

Another good thing about the past few weeks is that we're making good progress on our relationship. Sure, feelings and emotions are flowing, but I think we're making real progress. Some might say that we're even becoming friends again. I don't know for sure, but I'm almost certain that we're turning a corner. If nothing else, we're taking baby steps in the right direction.

It's great to watch TJ work the top water lure we use for bass fishing. I have to admit, it's my favorite fishing toy of them all. When worked properly, fish will literally jump on the hook. Of course, the real secret isn't the lure so much as the speed of the return. Go too fast, and the fish won't pay you any attention. Go too slow, and the lure doesn't do anything worthwhile. Hit the perfect blend, and you've got the fish off their normal routines, plotting and anticipating what to do next. Then, you have them. It's funny how fishing imitates life so distinctly in every way.

I remember teaching him the right rhythm when he was younger. He would get so frustrated at first, but he was a quick learner and soon got the hang of it. It seems to be our way with everything. After he mastered the technique, I took him fishing with me, but I told him that I would keep all the dumb fish, and he could keep all the smart ones. He agreed, and it took two or three fish before he caught on—as I kept telling him that the smart ones don't get caught that easily and took his fish.

Funny, it was actually similar to the way my father introduced me to catching crappy. We started out early one morning to get to the right spot a friend had told him about. It's very important to find the right spot when catching crappy because they're creatures of habit. I was probably around eleven years old at the time, and I considered myself a pretty good fisherman; however, this was my first time to fish for crappy.

My father always liked to make bets, so we made a bet as to who would catch the most crappy. If he won, I had to wash his car; and if I won, he had to take out the trash for a week. I was pumped because I wasn't going to let him win. We trolled the boat near the bank and put the anchor down about ten feet from an old tree that had fallen in the water. We fixed our poles, adjusted the drag, and cast our lines. Our floats set up on the water, and we waited for the game to begin.

I was the first to get a bite, and as I had been taught from the first time I started fishing, I jerked the pole back and set the hook like a pro. The result was nothing but an empty hook staring back at me when I reeled it in. A few moments later—another bite—same result. My father just laughed at me.

Soon, he reeled his line in with a nice, one-pound crappy on the end. He carefully took the fish off the hook and smiled at me as he tossed him into the live well.

"Don't give up. You'll get one," he said sarcastically.

"I'm not giving up."

A few minutes later, he reeled in his second fish, his third, and then, his fourth. As for me, I was at my wit's end. I was getting bites, but I couldn't catch anything. After his fifth catch, I was done and ready to accept defeat.

"Oh, you can't give up now. We've only been here for an hour," he said.

"I don't care. I can't catch anything. I'm getting bites, and you're catching all the fish. I'm mad about it."

It was at this point that a huge grin came over his face and he chuckled as he spoke. "Oh yeah, there's one thing I forgot to mention. Crappy have very soft skin around their mouths, so if you jerk the pole too hard to set the hook like you do with other fish, you'll pull the hook straight through their mouths. You need to let them swallow the hook before you gently set it."

If looks could kill, he would've been gone. He just laughed and laughed at me, and as hard as I tried, I couldn't keep my smile in, but I wasn't about to wash anybody's car. We had a really good time the rest of that day, and yes, he caught the most fish. Of course, once he started with a five to nothing lead, he should have.

As I drift back to the present, I must have been smiling because I hear TJ's voice in my ear. "Dad, what are you thinking about?" he asked.

"Your grandpa and one of his practical jokes. It's no wonder I need therapy."

"What was it? What did he do?" he asked, setting his pole down, turning to listen.

I tell him the whole story and maybe even embellish it a little bit. I'm not ashamed to admit it—it is a fish story after all. When I finish, he laughs pretty hard.

"Kind of reminds me of those smart fish, dumb fish," he said.

"Yes, it kind of does. Hey, you probably need some therapy, too."

We sit there for awhile just remembering those times. We each have a smile on our face, so they must have been good ones. It's nice to be in this place again, as it seems that we never are anymore. The way it goes…we'll probably be fighting by nightfall.

"Dad," TJ said.

"Yes."

"Do you ever wonder what it would be like to be rich?"

"Sometimes, I guess. I don't think about it as much as I used to."

"Do you ever just sit back and think about why fortune never came your way?"

"I don't know. Why are you hammering me with these questions?"

"I'm not trying to hammer you," he said. "I'm just wondering what it would be like to be rich and powerful, and I'm curious if you've ever felt the same way."

"Like I missed out?"

"Something like that. When you say it like that, it makes it sound so harsh."

I know what he means from the first question, but I don't necessarily want to get back into why I haven't done more with my life. I know it's probably my own stuff coming up, but I don't care. When did it become okay to kick somebody when he's down? I don't think it's good, and I'm not sure that I want to go there.

"Why do you want to be rich and powerful?"

"Because, then I could get my way whenever I wanted. People would have to respect my wishes if I had enough money to make things happen."

"Interesting theory, I have to say."

"Well, I think it would work well," TJ said. "Don't you?"

"There's a lot to be said about always getting your way, and years ago, I would've agreed with you completely, even though I've never had the pleasure of being rich; however, I think your logic might be just a little off."

"How so?"

"When I said earlier that in the past, I often thought about being rich and powerful, I meant it. That was my goal for the longest time, and I bounced from one get-rich-quick scheme to another. But, I learned a valuable lesson."

"What is it?" TJ asked before I can finish.

"The lesson is that you can be rich and not powerful, and you can be powerful and not rich. Then, there are the very few who are both rich and powerful."

"Huh?"

I can see my reasoning is completely lost on him, based on the puzzled look on his face. Much like his question of wealth in the beginning, he wants glitz and glamour, not ordinary. Having walked in his shoes, I know what he's thinking and even what he wants. Unfortunately, he hasn't walked in my shoes, so he doesn't understand what I'm thinking and what I've seen. Sometimes, experience offers the best guidance. Other times, its realistic view can dampen the spirit because you tend to know where it's going to end, and unfortunately, there are no romantic outcomes.

"TJ, a rich man can certainly buy any thing that he wants, and to me, that would be a great thing. But, having money to buy things doesn't provide you with anything but stuff. I say this because you can't buy things like love, respect, and honor. Do you know why?"

"No," TJ answered, bracing himself for another talk.

"Because love, respect, and honor are words of power. They come from the soul and you can't buy them. You have to earn them, and once you do, you have to show them to others all the time."

"So, what makes the difference?"

"In a nutshell, faith-based humility."

"What the heck is that?"

"It's something that you, me and everyone should try to live by and understand. It means that we should recognize that we aren't the center of the universe—that we're just a piece of it. It means that we're directly responsible for our actions and that we have to have enough humility to pride ourselves in treating others with kindness, respect and love all the time."

"That all sounds great, Dad, but really, what does it have to do with power?"

"Everything."

"How?"

"Son, think about it. There are things in your life that you have control over and there are many things that you don't. You can work your whole life to try and be rich, successful, and powerful; yet, never get there because it's out of your control. You should know that if you don't make it, then it's okay because as I've said before, money can't buy you what you're looking for. What you're looking for is already inside you and a part of who you are. You have the power now."

"What power?" TJ asked in disbelief. "What power can I possibly have now?"

"TJ, you're not listening to me."

"I am too!"

"No, you're not. Close your eyes and empty your mind."

"What?"

"Just do it…Now, listen to what I'm saying, and don't say anything. Let your mind just take it all in."

"Fine," TJ said as he reluctantly closes his eyes.

"Here are a couple of things that give you the power you are looking for. You have the power to love, the power to lead; the power to learn, and the power to teach; the power to be honest, and the power to forgive; the power to be free, and the power to serve; the power to give, and the power to have faith.

"TJ, that's true power. If you spend your energy making yourself better than you are and giving to others, then true power will be yours, and you will reap the benefits of success and money. But, if you spend your energy in search of money and success, you may find it, but you won't have true power."

"I'm sorry, Dad, but this isn't working for me."

Why is he fighting me on this? I can't make him understand. Maybe I'm not doing a good job of explaining it to him. I don't know, but I'm doing the best I can to make it make sense. I'm not being critical of rich people. Hell, quite the opposite—I wish I had money. I've just seen how it can change a person and usually not for the better. It was a hard lesson for me to learn. I guess it's that damn Phillips' hard-headedness, that we both share, getting in the way.

"Dad, a couple of questions. What makes you the authority on this?" TJ asked. "No offense, but you've never been rich, so how would you know if they have true power or not?"

"I'm not claiming to be the authority on this or anything else anymore. I'm just giving you insight into something I've lived through and come to understand. I may not have the flashy style you're looking for or the money to buy people's affections, but I do know about being responsible because I've lived it my whole life. I'm learning humility every moment of every day, it seems, and as I've said before, once you understand both of these things, then true power is yours."

"I'm trying to get it, but it's tough."

"I know it is, Son, and I understand completely how you feel. I've been there—not just with this—but with most everything. One day, a light will go on and you'll understand what I'm trying to say. One day, it'll become crystal clear, like it did for me. You'll start to look inward for what you seek. When you do, it'll be a great day because on that day, your life will change. Always remember that you can't find inner peace by looking outward."

We sit back and enjoy the afternoon and the fishing. I guess, since there are no fights going on, we're having a good day. I wish we could talk like this all the time because we can learn a lot from each other. TJ is trying, and I'm grateful. How do I teach him something that only experience and time can bring? Why does he have to wait until he's my age to realize that he can command power within himself? What a great gift it would've been if I had listened so long ago. Missed opportunities make up a majority of my life so far. Humility, it appears, will be my greatest teacher.

15 EARL AND TIM ARRIVE ON THURSDAY EVENING before the Fourth of July fishing tournament. With the Fourth falling on Saturday this year, Friday is the day most people have off from work. Earl decides the drive and the fishing will be worth it.

I've been looking forward to the big weekend because I've missed being around Earl. Next to Jen, he knows me best, and we can talk about anything. Mainly, I'm just missing home more than I can admit, but as I've come to understand, some sacrifices are necessary.

Once they arrive, TJ and Tim immediately head into town to whatever place TJ likes to go. Watching them together is interesting because they share a bond that's like brothers. I would love to be a fly on the wall and listen in on their conversations. I'm sure Earl and I would be kept in the highest regard.

Earl and I have bigger plans—raiding the cooler for some pilsner refreshments before dinner. Our plan for the weekend is simple—just fish until we can't fish anymore and win the tournament. The tournament is a two-day event starting Friday and ending on Saturday night with a Fourth of July celebration and fish fry. The rules call for each team to catch a total of ten yellow perch over the two-day period, determine the combined weight of the catch, and then compare it to the others. The winning team gets prize money of one thousand dollars and bragging rights for the summer.

The weather is unseasonably cool for this time of year, and the locals predict that we'll have a hard time catching yellow perch. They believe that the cooler temperatures will cause the perch to feed closer to the top of the water than they usually do. Usually, the yellow perch stay deep in the cool water during the summer months. Who knows? Nonetheless, it should be fun.

I invite Earl out to sit with me on my porch sanctuary, and he agrees. We talk for most of the afternoon and into the night.

"So, how's everything going?" Earl asked.

"It's going okay. Some days have been better than others, but all in all, not too bad. For the most part, I've been to the well and back, but it's good."

"That's good. When I spoke to you a few weeks ago, you said you had really started to figure it all out—at least with TJ."

"Earl, I've got to be honest with you. When we spoke before, I really thought I had found an insight into things, but I quickly realized that I don't know anything."

"Really?" Earl asked in disbelief. "It sure sounded to me like you had it all under control."

Control. Yeah, there's that word again. We all toss it around like some ball we found on the street. Here, you take it. No, I want it back. Whoever has the ball has the control, and we all want the ball. It's funny that Earl mentions control because it's obvious that my controlling nature got me into this place in my life. All it's taught me is that I'm sure as hell not going to pretend to know anything going forward, and I'm only commenting on what I've seen and come to believe.

"I've found my way as the weeks have gone by, but that's about it. I planned this trip to get away, fish, and be alone; then Jen sends TJ with me. So, I figured I would use this time to set him straight on a few things. The sad thing is that I've realized that I'm the one that needs to be fixed, and it's not easy to take when you figure that out."

"I had no idea you've been going through all that. I mean, I know you came here to take some time to deal with the loss of your dad and maybe get closer with TJ, but I guess I never thought it would be so hard."

"Apparently, I have many demons."

"Sounds like it," Earl said shaking his head. "Had a chance to face them all?"

"I don't know. It seems like a new one pops up everyday, but I've decided that it's nothing that a few good rounds of shock therapy won't cure."

"Have you tried my remedy?"

"What's that?"

"Beer therapy. After several of these, I promise that your problems will go away."

Friendship is such a beautiful thing—no pretense, just honesty. "Well, at least in the short-term anyway."

We sit back and talk about many things. I tell him everything that has happened to me since I've been here, including my breakdown and the visits from my father. I figure—why not? What's one more embarrassing moment in my life? Apparently, foolishness breeds embarrassment, or maybe I'm just a fool whose lot in life is to be the court jester for others. It doesn't matter anymore, and I've got nothing more to hide.

Friday morning comes way too early for the four of us. I wish Earl and Tim could've come up a couple of days earlier, so we could've fished the different spots that TJ and I have found. If so, then all of us would be more familiar with what to expect this weekend. Sure, Earl's been here before and he told me about this place, but he only came for a few days, and that was a pretty good while ago.

I'm not really too worried about it because both Earl and Tim are good fishermen, so we should be fine. Heck, if we don't do well, it doesn't matter since this tournament is more about bragging rights than it is for money. My competitive nature just wants to beat Mike and the boys if for no other reason than to rub it in. That's when you know you've got good friends—when you make fun of them and give them hell when you beat them at something. It makes life so much more fun, and honestly, they'd do it to you.

Since we've got a two-day tournament and a ten fish limit, there's also some strategy that must be used in order to assure ourselves a good showing, and hopefully, a victory. The rules of the tournament state that there are two weigh-ins—one Friday night, and the other, Saturday night. So, there is the possibility that some teams may catch ten fish the first day, weigh-in, and be done by Friday night.

Personally, I think that's a terrible strategy for several reasons. First, you would spend your entire Saturday waiting for the inevitable to happen—a team weighing-in, beating your mark, and rubbing it in your face. Next, you would miss the opportunity to go out and fish, compete and have fun on the water for an extra day, which is a true fisherman's wish. Finally, all fishermen know that there is a wall-mounting, monster of a fish just waiting to be caught, and what better time to do it than in a tournament with cash and bragging rights on the line?

My father taught me that any pre-fishing tournament conversation should be regarded as basic trash. Your 'friends' will give you advice on where to catch the 'mother load' of fish because just yesterday, they had fished that spot and couldn't get the hook in the water fast enough. This is why I love having Earl with me at tournaments. One glance at the lake map and Earl has a few spots he can reel off in a friendly verbal exchange. He also has the uncanny ability to blend into any environment, no matter where he is.

"Tom, good morning," Mike said, as he makes his way across the parking lot. "Who do you have with you?"

"Mike, this is my good friend, Earl, and his son, Tim."

"Earl, good to meet you."

"You too," Earl replied.

"I hate that we're meeting under these circumstances," Mike said with a grin.

"What do you mean?"

"Well, I hate that you've come all this way to fish in the tournament with Tom. I've seen him and TJ fish. It's not pretty," Mike said with a loud, hearty laugh.

"I'll take my chances."

Like I said—you know you've got good friends when they 'dog' you to others. We've definitely got to beat these guys. Mike and the boys have won this tournament for four straight years.

As we get settled into the boat and start out in the morning air, a misty fog covers the lake; however, visibility isn't too bad. All four of us are bundled up like we're ready to go ice fishing in the dead of winter, but we all know it's a matter of time before the sun starts to shine and the day really gets going.

Earl and I had carefully examined the lake map the night before, and we had marked the areas where TJ and I had the most luck. We also decide that we'll keep just four fish today and take our chances on Saturday trying to catch the rest. We're a little concerned about the cooler weather, but everybody has that same problem.

We catch a couple of fish early. Surprisingly, Tim hauls in the first catch of the day, and I follow quickly after with a nice catch of my own. TJ seems disappointed that he doesn't catch the first fish, but he does seem glad for Tim. I remind him that the team is the most important thing to remember, but apparently, that isn't the best thing to say since all he does is quickly cut his eyes my way and scowl.

Around lunchtime, things are all quiet on the fishing front. Other than being the hottest part of the day, I think the locals are right about the cooler water temperatures because we haven't caught anything in awhile. I don't think we've found the right depth just yet, and we may be lucky to catch the four fish we want today.

The weigh-in is scheduled between five and six o'clock, and by three, we have nothing more than the two fish we caught this morning. After discussing with Earl about changing the depth of our casts and moving to another spot where TJ and I had success before, we get lucky. Earl catches two nice-sized perch right before we have to head back for the weigh-in. Somebody must have been smiling on us because we're able to keep with our overall strategy.

Most teams have between four and six fish to weigh. One team has eight, and another has three, but everybody else stays consistent. The official weight of our first day catch: six pounds, five ounces. We are in fifth place overall and more than four pounds behind the leader, Mike's team, who has weighed-in with six fish.

There isn't any trash talking as the teams come into weigh. Actually, there's very little conversation at all among the guys. Apparently, everyone feels it was a tough day to catch anything, and we're all tired and hungry. TJ is disappointed that he didn't catch anything, but he and Tim are in their own little world, so I know he's having a good time.

Saturday morning is almost a replica of the day before, with the exception being that we can't get a bite, much less catch anything. We move from spot to spot throughout mid-morning until around noon, but we still have no luck. We're trying nearly every spot that TJ and I had been fishing for a couple of months, yet nothing.

During lunch, Earl and I are looking at the map and trying to figure our next move. So far, our predetermined hot spots have been ice cold.

"Dad," said TJ.

"Yes."

"How about Brown's Cove?"

"Well, I don't know. It would be a longshot."

"What's Brown's Cove?" Earl asked.

"It's a place that's a little removed from the normal fishing spots. TJ and I have fished there about three times since we've been here. We've had mediocre luck there at best."

"Hell, mediocre is a lot better than we've got now," Earl said. "Do you think the others have tried it?"

"No, I doubt it. Fred told us about it when we got here," TJ replied. "I think he was trying to be our friend."

"Since we don't know the layout of the lake, Tim and I are going to leave it up to you two," Earl said.

"I'm not sure if it's worth trying. TJ, what do you think?"

"I say we try it. What do we got to lose? We gain an extra hour with the two-hour weigh-in tonight, and that'll give us plenty of time to get there and back."

"I'm in," said Earl.

"Me too," said Tim.

"Then, let's do it."

I watch TJ closely as my words linger in the air, and we pull anchor and make preparations for Brown's Cove. He's happy and grinning, which is great to see. It isn't the kind of grin where he's self-satisfied and gloating; rather, it's a grin of empowerment and knowing that his opinion matters to us all—especially me.

We arrive at Brown's Cove with about two hours of fishing time before we have to head back. We all make the decision to fish a depth of around fifteen feet and hope for the best. We get a few nibbles at first, and then we catch two. TJ catches the first one, and I quickly follow with the next. Each of them is a definite keeper. Within the hour, we had caught two more and needed another two to have our ten. Sure, we would love to have the luxury of throwing some back and keeping the big ones, but to just get to ten will be worth it in this tournament.

Earl catches the fifth one of the day, and we're one short. From what we can tell, all the fish are average or a little above average in size and weight. Pooled together, the final weight will most likely not be enough to win, but we at least had some fun and got to spend this time together.

With a short amount of time to go before we have to head back, we're all fishing like maniacs. We get a nibble here and a nibble there, but we can't hook that one last fish. Personally, I'm hoping for some divine intervention to make a fish just jump on a hook and get us to ten because God knows I've sacrificed enough lures in my lifetime that it should happen.

"Whoa!" TJ suddenly yelled.

"What is it?"

"Something just grabbed this thing, and I think it's big."

We all stop and lay our poles down as he speaks. Earl and I start looking for signs to see if the fish is about to surface, and Tim grabs the net.

"Bring him in slow and easy. Don't reel when he takes off."

"I'm trying!"

"Let him tire himself out. We've got time."

TJ does a masterful job of working the reel. He lets the fish jerk and move, then once it stops to rest, he slowly reels him in a little more. The whole process takes about twenty minutes to complete. He probably could have gotten him in quicker, but TJ doesn't want to lose this fish, so he takes his time. Earl and I can see that it is a yellow perch and that it's bigger than any of the other fish we had caught so far. But we can't get a good look at it until TJ has him close to the boat. One swoop of the net, and Tim has him captured. TJ has his fish.

"My God, look at that monster!" said Earl.

"You're the man, TJ!" screamed Tim.

"Damn son! That's the biggest yellow perch I've ever seen! It even rivals the one in the picture at Fred's store. It's got to be more than two pounds, easy."

We pull anchor and go wide open back to the dock for the final weigh-in. TJ grins from ear to ear. I'm so glad he's the one who caught the big fish and not me. I'm so proud of him for sticking with it and not getting upset when things weren't going well for him early on. It also makes me realize that all of the accomplishments that I've earned or achieved in my life mean nothing to me when compared to a huge grin on TJ's face after a big moment in his life. That's the true beauty of life that I'm coming to understand—watching my kid do special things, being proud of him, seeing his smile light up, and knowing that he's the most important thing.

At the final weigh-in, the guys on each team are standing around and watching the scoreboard for changes. Everyone is waiting to see who's coming in, and they're placing small wagers on who will win. Not to mention, everyone is ready for the big Fourth of July fish fry and celebration.

When we pull our catch out to be weighed, the crowd quickly gathers around—especially since we're the next to last team to come in. The crowd gives a huge roar of applause when TJ's fish is presented. It weighs two pounds, nine ounces—one of the largest yellow perch caught in a long time, and the second largest ever caught in the state. TJ is called up to the stage and given the biggest fish trophy and the one hundred-dollar prize, which none of us knew anything about.

Later that night at the fish fry celebration, we're having a great time. TJ and Tim take off to be with TJ's girlfriend and her friends while Earl and I settle in at my usual spot with Mike and the boys. We eat and drink as much as we possibly can, and since we came in second to Mike's team by only three ounces, we're ribbed a great deal. Of course, this means that we've gained a great deal of respect among the guys, and we're solidified as locals from then on.

When the music stops for a moment, Bob Wilson comes over to me for a quick conversation. Ever since TJ and I went out on his boat a couple of months ago, Bob and I had become pretty good friends.

"Tom," said Bob.

"Hey, Bob, how are you?"

"Good, thanks. Hey, I just wanted to let you know that you have a great son, and he's a hell of a fisherman."

"Thanks."

At this, Bob walks away, and I find myself trying to figure out what he said and what he meant by it. Sure, it's great to hear how wonderful you kid is from others, but I just wish I knew why he said it.

"What did he say?" Earl asked.

"Just something really nice about TJ."

"I'm sure he won't be the last one to do so," Earl said, as he raises his drink to me in respect.

16

I READ IN THE PAPER RECENTLY WHERE A GROUP of the town's teenagers had been busted for drugs. I know TJ sometimes hangs out with these kids, and my first concern is that he might know something or worse, he's been a part of what they're into. I'm also concerned that he might think I'm prying into his privacy and don't trust him if I ask him some questions about it.

How do we talk with our kids about drugs, alcohol and other addictions? Who has the answers? If somebody does, I'd like to sit down with him and get some pointers. Nobody gives you a manual on how to raise kids, so how do you know what to do?

You have this euphoria that overcomes you when you find out that you're going to be a parent, but then you start worrying and stressing over every detail of the pregnancy. Then, you find yourself praying for a healthy child at every open moment you have. But you know, deep down, that you're ready to accept whatever God gives you, and that it's bigger than you are.

You feel relieved when you count ten fingers and ten toes, but then another set of stressors find their way into your mind and it starts all over again. There is no peace in being a parent because you're constantly on alert—worried something out of your control may happen. Eventually, you learn to deal with it, and accept that you've been blessed by this miracle in your life, and you move on—at least until your kid starts walking.

For me, there's not a greater moment in early parenthood than when TJ took his first steps. At that moment, he was no longer a baby—he was a little boy, full of energy and ready for trouble. Sure, some people would argue that a baby's first smile or his first words are the best, and I'd have to agree to some extent that they're correct. Although it wasn't the first word he spoke, when TJ said 'Da Da' for the first time, I cried a soft, happy cry, and I'm not ashamed to admit it. I do, however, have to draw the line with the first smile. I know it's a wonderful and beautiful thing, but being the cynic that I am, I could never tell if TJ was smiling because he was happy, or if he was smiling because he had gas. I always thought it was funny and a great observation on my part, but Jen never gave me much credit for it.

TJ has grown up so fast, and it seems like yesterday when we were playing trains together. Where did the time go? Where did he go? Hell, where did I go? My hope is that he's developed a true sense of himself, and we've given him a solid foundation he can rely on as he gets older and faces more things. It's just like these teenagers busted for drugs. They're out there doing this and doing that, and their parents think everything is fine. Then—BAM! In an instant, everything crashes down and those fears you've kept hidden inside for a long time come out and bite you in the ass. We, as parents, can't control what our kids do when they're faced with temptations. All we have is our hope, and we pray with every ounce of our being that it doesn't happen to our kids.

What should I do about this article I read? Should I bring it up, or just let it go? TJ and I have been getting along so well lately, and I don't want to screw that up. We haven't been this close in a long time, and I like being here with him and hanging out, talking about guy stuff. We're becoming friends again, and that's important to me. What to do?

Later that afternoon, I hear TJ coming into the cabin. He sounds like he is in a pretty good mood. He's whistling, so I figure he's in a good place.

"TJ, is that you?"

"Yes," he answered. "Where are you?"

"Where I always am—on the porch."

"I had no doubt," he said sarcastically. "What have you been doing out here? I'm sure it's been most of the afternoon."

"Thinking."

"You seem to do a lot of that lately."

"You have no idea. What about you, where've you been?"

"I was out with my friends. We've been hanging out around town, goofing off. It was fun."

"Cool. Glad you enjoyed it. Hey, I've got a question for you, but I don't know if I should ask you or not."

"Okay, hit me!"

"TJ, I don't know the best way to say this, so I'm just going to say it."

"What is it?" TJ asked, his playfulness becoming serious.

"I read the article in the paper about Mickey and Josh getting busted for drugs, and..."

"And you think I'm involved, don't you?"

"Son, let me finish."

"What's there to finish? I can't believe you. First of all, it was just pot, not hardcore drugs like everybody thinks; and second, they were set up by Mickey's girlfriend's dad."

"Now, you wait a damn minute and let me finish what I was going to say. I'm not accusing you of being involved, and it doesn't matter whether it was just pot or not—drugs are drugs. Besides, I was trying to have a conversation with you, man to man."

TJ locks his gaze on me as I speak and his look tells me more than I really want to know about what he's thinking.

"I wanted to talk about what happened and how you feel about it—things like that. But apparently that's a waste since you can't be calm."

"What? Honestly, I can't believe you. So, you just wanted to talk about things and have me tell you everything? Is that what you thought?"

"Yes."

"Do you think I'm an addict or something? Do you think I will tell you, so you can tell me what I need to do to fix it—so you can control it?"

"No, I don't think you're an addict or anything like that. I thought you would want talk with me."

"Why would you think that? What do you think gives you the right to ask me about anything?"

"Because I'm your father."

"My Father? Where were you when I had questions that I wanted answers to? Where were you when I was dealing with things that were tough for me to handle? Mom was there. Where were you?"

"TJ, I…"

"Never mind, I don't care. You know what? I'm done. I don't want to hear your excuses and how you messed up. I think we both can agree on that," he said, standing up and heading for the door. "For your information, I've never done any drugs whatsoever. It was offered to me, but I turned it down. Are you happy?"

With his last comment, TJ opens the door into the cabin and slams it shut behind him. I don't have the courage to go after him because everything he said was true. What right do I have and where was I when he needed me? I can't move, so I just sit on the porch for the rest of the afternoon—thinking—the thing I do best.

Eventually, I turn my chair to face the lake, and I watch as the sun begins to set across the water. I can't help but think that another day, which started out so great, is now lost yet again. I curl my lip into a disappointed frown and take in a deep breath. Life sucks sometimes. It just does.

But, as I watch the power of the setting sun at dusk, and I take in the calming beauty of the scene, the truth reveals itself to me. I don't want to be his friend if that's all I can get. I want to be his father. I can tell that I've gotten through to him, and I know he feels it even though he's angry with me.

Of course, he's not going to like my asking about his business, and he's right about my not being there for him in the past. I have no excuses anymore; but dammit, I'm his father whether he likes it or not, and I'm going to ask him the tough questions, and he's going to answer them.

I've sat on this freaking porch and wallowed in my shortcomings for far too long. I can't do it anymore. I've thought about my life, my family, and my own mortality, and the answers have come in bits and pieces. Are we here to learn lessons in our life? If we don't, then do we keep repeating the same old cycles over and over? What happens if we learn those lessons and change our lives for the better? Is it over then? Do we finally have peace?

When I came here in the spring, I was a mess. My relationship with my son sucked. I was unhappy with my job, and I was a major control freak who always had to have everything my way. My father had just died, and the only thing keeping me going—Jen—was sick of me and wanted a break.

Now, months later, I've searched the depths of my soul and examined myself completely. I've looked in the mirror and shed tears for the person staring back at me. I've felt the emptiness, pitied myself, and poured everything I had out on the table. Truly, I've been beaten down again and again. I have nothing left to feel sorry about, because I have nothing left, period. I know it's time for me to get off my ass and make it right from now on, and I'm going to do that starting right now.

I jump out of my chair and head straight into TJ's room. When I get there, he's lying on the bed reading a magazine. He looks up at me, and I can tell some of his anger has gone, but I know he's still mad.

"TJ, I want you to listen to me, and I don't want you to say anything, okay?"

TJ closes his magazine and shuffles himself to a sitting position on the bed, but he doesn't speak.

"I'm very proud of you for never trying any kind of drugs. I didn't know if you had or not, but I'm so glad you haven't. I'm just like every other parent who is afraid of what might happen to his child. From the day you were born, I've worried about things in your life that I can't control. I know that temptation is always around because I've either been there and seen it, or worse, I've made those mistakes myself."

I pause and watch for a reaction, but TJ isn't about to give in just yet. I hate it when he acts like me.

"I don't care about the circumstances surrounding Mickey and Josh. All I care about is that you weren't involved and that you're okay. I know what their parents are feeling right now, and it's not good. It's sickness and true sorrow. I'm not perfect, and you know that. I have no excuse for not being there for you earlier in your life, but I'm here now, and I am your father. I'm also going to start acting like it from now on—not just going through the motions."

I can see TJ's eyes getting moist and swollen from trying to hold back tears, but he doesn't let go. He's tough.

"Have you ever done drugs?" TJ asks directly.

"Once, when I was thirteen. I went over to a friend's house with two other guys. My friend's parents were away, and we had the place to ourselves. The friend who lived there pulled out a joint from his private collection and lit it up. It was passed around, and we all took a hit off it. I was so ashamed of myself that I went back into the house and left them outside."

"Why were you ashamed?"

"Because, I let peer pressure dictate a moment of my life, and I made a bad choice. I've made many bad choices in my life since then, but I vowed right then that I would never do any drugs for the rest of my life, and I've kept my promise to myself. It's been offered to me a lot even from people I wouldn't have expected, but just like you, I turned it down. That's why I'm proud of you—because you made a good choice for yourself."

"Dad, why is it that in a situation like with Mickey and Josh, everybody immediately thinks they're addicts? You've met them, and you know they're both good guys. Sure, they got messed up in some stuff, but c'mon, they're not addicts."

"I don't really know how to answer that. Honestly, I don't. My guess would be that as a society, we rush to call someone out when his mistakes are made public. Doing so, makes us feel better about ourselves and allows us to mask our own demons."

"How so?"

"Well, for starters, I've come to realize that we're all addicted to something, and we have the propensity to fall deeper into the abyss of that addiction if we don't recognize it and take steps to correct it."

"We all have… addictions?"

"I think so."

"Do you mean like drugs and alcohol, stuff like that?"

"Yes, those are obvious ones, but not everyone does drugs or drinks. Other addictions are things like smoking, gambling, sex, and food. Hell, the list is endless."

"What's your addiction?"

"Mine's a little different, but still an addiction. You may not know this about me, but I'm a Type-A control freak."

Finally, I get a smile from him as he looks up and says, "Who, you? I would have never guessed."

"Yep, it's true. I think it's something that just started, and I'm pretty sure it's only temporary."

"You're right. It has been an adjustment for me getting used to these new controlling ways of yours."

"We can laugh about it because I'm finally owning it about myself, but it's as much an addiction as drugs, alcohol, or anything else. At first glance, you think it's not that bad because the consequences seem so different, but are they really?"

"Huh? I don't get it."

"Think about it. If I'm doing drugs or drinking all the time, I could do some things that could make me ultimately lose everything—my house, my job, or even my family. I could really hurt a lot of people, right?"

"Yeah."

"Well, if I'm a control freak, who always has to have my way, then I can still lose all of those things right?"

"Sure," TJ answered. "But I haven't seen too many control freaks hurt someone else. I mean, they don't drive under the influence, crash their car, and hurt innocent people. At least, I've never heard that report on the news—he was arrested for DWCF, Driving While Control Freak, and lost control of the car and slammed into the on-coming minivan. Police gave him a field test at the scene, but he insisted on making up his own rules and failed miserably."

TJ is laughing a little bit when he finishes. He feels like he is too smart, and he takes pride in it. It's pretty creative, I have to admit, but it's not something to take lightly. I would know—I am one.

"That's pretty funny, but try this scenario out, and see if it's still funny."

"Okay."

"Let's say there's this guy who's addicted to control, and he has a son. He spends all of his time telling his son what to do and making plans for him. He gets frustrated and stops being around when his son needs him. The days turn into weeks; the weeks turn into months; and the months turn into years. Then, one day, the guy realizes what he's done and tries to change. But, the damage has been done and the son sits and wonders—why now? You tell me, has an innocent person been hurt?"

TJ's smile quickly fades as my words finish ringing in his ears. His blank stare comes back, and it's obvious, he knows the story all too well. Dammit, I hate it when I do things like this to him. I wish I could take it like a man instead of resorting to these mean and childish tactics.

"That's not funny, Dad."

"I know, Son, and I'm sorry."

"It's okay," TJ said trying to reassure himself.

"No, it's not. I'm really sorry."

"Dad, it's okay. Tell me what addiction I have?"

"Only you can determine that. I would say, based on family history, you certainly have the potential to be an ass like your grandfather... and me. Hopefully, you've got enough of your mother's sweetness in you to balance things out."

"So, you really believe that we all have an addiction of some sort?"

"I do. I have no scientific proof to back it up. All I have is observation of those around me and careful reflection of my own life. That's why I think it sucks that anybody should be publicly called an addict by someone else when we all have problems. No one should be called out unless that person calls himself out first. I think Mickey and Josh are good boys that got mixed up in stuff that they shouldn't have been doing, but the fact is, they're the ones that made those choices and now they have to pay the consequences. I don't think it's fair to them to be labeled as addicts because none of us really know what's going on with them right now. We just have to hope and pray that they're going to be alright."

As always, our conversation ends with an empty air of things left unsaid. I don't know if it's my expertise at really screwing up a moment, or if he's just refusing to hear me, but sometimes, we just don't communicate. Either way, he looks at me like he's thinking of how many ways I've screwed up his life, or worse, how stupid he thinks I am. I just don't know what I'm doing anymore. Fortunately, tomorrow is another day.

17

THE WATER IS CALM AND BEAUTIFUL TODAY, AS I fish the afternoon and take in the solitude I so enjoy. TJ is away with his friends this afternoon, so I think it's a great chance to enjoy some time doing what I love—fishing and watching the sunset on the lake at dusk. I can't help but think about the events so far, and I'm having the realization that it'll soon be gone.

Three weeks. Three weeks, and it's time for me and TJ to call it a summer and go home. Chances are, we'll never have the opportunity to be together like this again. It seems like yesterday that we were in the backyard playing catch. I remember looking at him then and thinking how much he had grown. He was only eight at the time, but it was upon me before I knew it. Now, he's almost sixteen and probably two years away from leaving home for college, never to return. In some respects, it seems like he's been with us forever, then hardly at all. Maybe it stems from the fact that we don't really remember life without him. Maybe not, but either way, it's tough to think about.

I feel ashamed of myself for giving Jen such a hard time about sending TJ here with me. I felt like she was punishing me for never being able to connect with him or some other sinister reason she had come up with to get back at me. It turns out, as with most things she does, she knew this trip would be therapeutic for us both, and I think she's right.

I admit, that as far as therapy goes, I'm definitely on the A-list for those needing it, and I've had my moments of introspection that would make many blush at the thoughts I've had. But, I think this trip, and this place, have helped to heal my soul more than I could've ever known that it would.

Coming here, I thought I was in control of my life and all those around me. I believed I was a lion among men—strong and ferocious to the last breath. I felt this way because I have an instinctual nature for survival, and I vowed to protect myself and those I love with all that I have. Then, I realized I was more like a monkey—cute and playful, but the more time you spend with me, the more likely I am to throw my shit at you.

It's funny. Not really a laughing funny, but more of a tragic funny, because it's not easy to wake up and realize that you're the emotional equivalent of a primate when you thought yourself to be the king of the jungle. I think I might be okay if it were something like an eagle, or a dolphin—something which appears to have a small semblance of a clue—but no, I'm not that lucky.

I'm plagued by the ironies in my life. My struggles reflect my unwillingness to learn from my mistakes, and my reluctance to have faith guide my way. Irony provides me the outward proof of my tortured inner soul, and its message must be heard. I guess I should feel lucky that I'm starting to realize this now, as I approach my thirty-seventh birthday, and not when I'm ninety and near the end. At least now, I have the ability to make a difference for myself and those around me.

How will I make that difference? What will I do? I honestly don't know. Yet another irony, I guess. But, I do know that like anything else, it must be taken day by day. I don't expect to have all the answers right away like I did before. I've come to believe that one of the greatest lessons in life is perseverance, so I think from now on, I'm going to try it.

I think by using Jen's compelling notion of surrender and combining it with the humility I've experienced recently, I'll become a better person. Couple those principals with perseverance, and my faith will only get stronger. It has to.

Is it a guarantee to success and happiness? HA!—I laugh at that. There are no guarantees in life. This is what my mixed up world has taught me. I've also come to realize that it's my fault for my personal failures in parenting, and it's not TJ's job to fix our relationship issues. How would he? How can I expect him to? I'm the parent, and it's my job to make it right—even if that means I have to give in and do it differently. Somehow, someway, I've got to stop teaching TJ all of the harmful things I've learned along the way and start giving him something positive to use, as he becomes a man. I love my son so much, and the change is mine to make.

I reel in my line for the last time of the day and sit back to watch the sunset. It's calm and surreal as the deep orange light glistens off the breaking swells. The shoreline trees cut a shadowy, black row against the softer orange backdrop of the sky, and the sun sits like a large and powerful ball of fire squarely between them.

The funny thing is that I used to wish for dusk to find that one moment of harmony in my life. Now, I'm noticing that I have those peaceful moments all through the day. I may never actually be able to recreate the raw beauty of the lake and the sunset at dusk in my soul, but I'm certainly going to try.

As I guide the boat into the slip, I feel at home with myself, and I want to spend time with TJ. I want my time alone, and I'll gladly take it whenever possible, but I must admit I miss him when he's not here with me.

Later that evening, I'm making dinner when TJ comes in. I can tell he isn't too happy, but he doesn't give me any indication he wants to talk, so I don't push it.

"TJ."

"Yes."

"Dinner is almost ready, so get washed up."

"Okay."

"How was your day?"

"Fine."

Fine. There's that word I've come to know and love. How are you? Fine. How about we go out tonight? Fine. How was the movie? Oh, it was fine. It's such a universal word that brings such hope and positive reinforcement. Oh yeah, I love it. It begs me to ask a question like— do you care if I strip down and go streaking through town? Fine. No emotion—no definitive existence that I can reason from it. It just is, and it bugs me like no other word. I figure I can spend the rest of my days on this earth emitting absolutely no emotion by limiting my answers to things like *fine*, *sure*, and *whatever*.

"Okay, glad the day went well. Is there anything…"

"Dad, not right now. I'm not in the mood," TJ said, as he stops me in mid-sentence.

I don't get upset with him because he doesn't sound mean when he cuts me off. He sounds down and sincere. I figure I'll let him come to me when he's ready to talk, and if he doesn't, I'm not going to pry.

We finish a quiet dinner, where we have little, if any, talking at all. After, I decide to take a night walk and take in the beauty of the stars, the moon, and the hot summer air. TJ, after cleaning the dishes, makes his way into his room and shuts the door. Obviously, he needs time to work out whatever it is that's bothering him.

The moon is full and the stars are shining. I stop to gaze for awhile and try to pick out constellations. Of course, when your astronomical intelligence is relegated to the Big and Little Dippers, stargazing doesn't really have a lot of meaning, and it doesn't last too long either.

As I make my way back into the cabin, I notice that TJ's bedroom door is open, but he isn't in there.

"TJ."

"Yeah."

"Are you on the porch?"

"Yep."

"What are you doing out there?"

"Thinking."

Irony. It's like so many other things I've come to discover recently—you can learn so much from it. Oh, you can try to avoid it, but its lessons will find you. You just have to be open to receiving and learning from it.

"I think you've come to the right place."

"You would know," TJ said with a forced smile. "I figured if you could spend months out here, maybe there was something to it, so I thought I'd give it a try."

"Well?"

"Not bad."

"I was looking at the stars during my walk, and I guess living in the city, like we do, we tend to forget just how many of them there are and how spectacular they can be."

"Did you see Orion?"

I immediately give him my are-you-serious look because he knows better than that when it comes to my stargazing skills.

"Oh, Big Dipper?"

"Okay, Galileo, let's just quit while we're ahead," I say flashing a quick grin at him. "Can you believe we've only got three weeks until it's time to go home?"

"No."

"Me either. It seems like just the other..."

"Dad," TJ said, as he catches me in mid-sentence.

"Yes."

"How do you know if you're in love?"

The reason just became clearer as to why he's upset tonight. I thought this day might come because we do live so far away and the reality of the situation was destined to chime in.

"Son, that's a tough question to answer. Something happen between you and Penny?"

"She's mad at me, and I don't know why. She says I don't ever do anything she wants to do. I don't know why she said that because I always ask her what she wants to do and then we do it," TJ said, as his voice begins to crack. "She told me she doesn't want to see me anymore. I don't understand why."

"And you think you love her?"

"I don't know. How would I know? I've never been in love, so how could I know what it feels like? All I know is that it hurts, and I can't stop thinking about her."

I forget sometimes how innocent we are in our youth. Just like TJ, we're all so ready to tackle the world with everything we've got, but the reality is that we don't have the knowledge or experience to tackle much of anything. So, we tend to fall on our face a lot and get banged up before we start to understand.

It's funny, because I can hear my father shouting things out to me, and it makes me want to say something stupid and insensitive like he would. I can hear him now—*don't worry about her, there are plenty of fish in the sea,* or *shake it off because it's only puppy love.* But, as I think about these statements, I can't help but believe how harmful they are to hear. What a complete denial of TJ's feelings for this girl, and I can't do that to him. I might not think it's love, but who am I to discredit what he's feeling?

"TJ, I understand completely how you feel."

"You do?"

"Yeah. I've been in a similar spot."

"Really? I always thought Mom was the only person you've loved."

"Ideally, yeah, you're correct, but I had several girlfriends before your mother and I met. We ended up together, but before her; I had breakups and the same empty, painful feeling you're having right now. Your mother went through the same things because it happens to everybody. It hurts, and it sucks, but it does get better."

"I'm not sure that it can."

"I think you'll be surprised. Let me throw something at you to think about for a minute and tell me if it makes sense."

"Okay."

"Let's say Penny feels for you like you feel for her. Maybe it's love—maybe it's not—but whatever it is, it's something strong you both share. Maybe, subconsciously, Penny got angry with you because she's trying to protect herself from getting more hurt when you leave in a few weeks. Her defenses kicked in and you got some sideways anger about not doing anything that she wants to do. When in reality, she's mad at you because you're going to leave soon."

TJ stops for a moment to let my words sink in. I want him to realize that sometimes people get angry with us and they don't even know why. It doesn't justify the behavior if they are mean or cruel, but it does offer a little insight into a situation, and it let's us know there may be more going on than we can see. Plus, it's easier to see when you're in my spot—on the outside looking in.

"Maybe you're right, Dad," TJ said. "I hadn't thought of it that way."

"I may be right, or I may be wrong. I'm not going to claim to have the right answers on any situation where a female is involved—no way—but it may be another way to look at things."

"Yeah, maybe, but you never did answer my question."

"What question?"

"How do you know if you're in love?" TJ asked. "What made it different with you and Mom compared to the other girlfriends?"

"That's two questions."

"Humor me. You know what I'm saying."

"I'll try to explain it, but love is tough to describe because it's different for everyone."

"Try me."

"The beginning of a new relationship is always great. You laugh, you talk, and you can't wait to spend time with each other. That first part is so euphoric, and you believe that nothing will ever penetrate the bond you're building between each other. Ultimately, it seems, something inevitably goes wrong, and it's over. Then, you're left in a state like you're in right now—hurt and confused. It's a place that no one wants to be because once you've been there, you don't forget.

"Your Mom was different. As I mentioned before, we did all the things that new couples do, and each day, I couldn't wait to make up an excuse to either see her or call her on the phone. I had signed up for the Marines a week before I met her, so we both knew that I would be leaving a few months after we met. Sound familiar?"

"Yeah."

"Those three months were some of the best months of my life—right up until two weeks before I was set to leave for boot camp. That's when your mother broke up with me."

"What?"

"Yep, she did. She said I was too suffocating for her and that I was too closed off. She also said that she didn't want to see me anymore. I was devastated and hurt, and I just kept thinking about all the time we had spent together and how great it was for us both. I didn't think that I was too overbearing on her, but I guessed I must have been."

"What did you do?"

"I spent the next twelve days in my room thinking I had lost someone special in my life, and I knew I was leaving for a long time. Then, I decided that I had to talk with her before I left because I had to know the truth. I summoned up the courage and went over to her house to speak with her."

"Then what?"

"I rang the doorbell, and your grandfather answered. As you know, we never got along that well in the beginning, but on that night, I wasn't going away."

"I bet that was wild!"

"Yeah, it was. My heart was pounding and finally he called your mother downstairs. My guess was that he knew I was serious and I wasn't going away without talking with her. He also probably figured that was the only way to get me to leave."

"Probably so."

"It was. Anyway, your mom and I spent the next three hours on the front porch talking. I told her how sorry I was for suffocating her in our relationship and how much our time together meant to me. She told me that I really hadn't been too overbearing, and that she had made all of that up. Instead, she confessed that she felt very deeply for me, and she didn't want to be more hurt once I left for boot camp. She also had made up her mind that I was going to forget all about her when I left."

"Really?"

"Yeah. So, we spent the entire next day together. I told her how much I loved her, and she told me how much she loved me."

"So, you just knew it then?"

"Well, no, not exactly."

"I don't understand."

"Like I said before, love is complicated and difficult to describe. See, we were still in that euphoric stage where everyone is happy, the feelings and emotions are high, and you're basically punch drunk with love. It hits you over the head, and you can't eat or sleep without thinking about the other person. You're probably at that place now aren't you?"

"Yeah," TJ answered. "So, you're saying that what I'm feeling isn't love, just a teenage love-struck crush?"

"No, no, no. What you're feeling is very real, and whether it's love or not is something you have to answer. But, I will tell you that there is so much more to being in love than what you might think there is."

"Like what?"

"Work, for starters."

"Work? What does work have to do with it?"

"Everything."

"Huh?"

"I said it before, and I'll say it again. I don't claim to have any expertise on relationships. I think we all start out trying to find that one special person put on this earth just for us. We meet people, date and have fun while trying to unlock the secret of happiness and love. Then, once we meet somebody special, we begin that euphoric high and start thinking to ourselves that this could be it—all we've ever wanted and dreamed about in another person. But, as with all things, the euphoria begins to fade and we struggle to keep the magic.

"This is where we've got to work at it to make it last. Sometimes, you get lucky, and it does, but most of the time, it doesn't. It's during this time, when we realize that we want more, that we begin to look for the things that were overshadowed when the relationship was rosy. We begin to take the relationship to the next level—to love."

"That sounds pretty simple."

"Simple? Son, have you ever been around a woman? There's nothing simple about it. Men can't even comprehend the complexities that women bring into a relationship. The lone hope is to be standing in the end."

TJ looks up at me, and we both burst out laughing. It's a good moment for us both. I roll my eyes in disbelief, and he just laughs some more.

"For me, being away from your mom was actually a good thing. Absence, does indeed, make the heart grow fonder."

"That's what they say," TJ said. "But doesn't it also give you time to think about things a little harder?"

"Yep, and in my situation, it was a good thing. It gave me time to figure out if I wanted to spend my life with your mother, and if I really was truly in love with her."

"What made you sure?"

"Well, I realized that the euphoria we had shared before I left was great, but it wasn't that feeling I missed. What I missed most about her were the little, intangible things that made her who she is. Things like her half-grin smile she has when she walks so gracefully into a room like everyone's been waiting for her to arrive, or how she can take a walk for fifteen minutes and get a tan. There are so many things—it's hard to name them all—but I love how she crunches her food when she eats; how our conversations are so real and deep; how she moves to a song when it comes on the radio; and how she jumps in fear when she sees a spider. To me, that's love."

"Sounds like you miss her."

"Yeah, I really do. TJ, I'm no expert, but I've been married a long time so I have some knowledge on the subject. Love is work, and it's not easy. When you find that special someone, you'll discover that you're willing to go through a lot to see if it's meant to be. Chances are, you'll find that it's worth the effort you need to put into it. Don't be afraid to try and find it because when you do, you'll be rewarded with great joy and happiness in your life. Times will be good, bad, and ugly. When they are and when you're in the middle of a tough stretch and not sure what to do, just think about those little, intangible things that made you fall in love in the first place. They're still there and all you have to do is look for them and remember."

"I guess my three months haven't been love, huh?"

"I don't know, buddy. Again, that's got to be your call to make. I would say that I wouldn't let anymore time be lost between you two. If she's the one for you, then over time and distance, it'll work out. If not, then you've had a great experience for a summer, and it'll help make you a better man. Now, I suggest that you get up tomorrow and go see Penny. Don't let her sideways anger keep you two from three more weeks of having fun together. Be honest with how you feel, and I think you'll find out that the truth is she's not really that angry with you, just scared and hurt."

"Okay, I will," TJ said with a renewed confidence. "Thank you, Dad."

"Anytime, Son. Anytime."

18

The morning comes early for us both, as it often had during our stay, but we start this day like almost all the others, ready to go.

"Dad," TJ said.

"Yes."

"I want to drive this morning."

The request to drive isn't that unusual because we've actually been practicing for a couple of months. TJ is about six months from his sixteenth birthday, and he does have a permit. So, I figured that since we were away from home, and he had no peer pressure to hurry and start driving, we would start slow and get plenty of practice. Besides, the town is very laid back and there isn't a lot of traffic, and I think those are the best conditions we could have.

"Okay."

I have to admit that it's a little odd that he wants to drive to the boat dock this morning, because usually, he's half asleep as we start out.

"So, what's going on?"

"Nothing."

He immediately turns away from me, so I'm guessing he's up to something. For the fun of it, I think I'll play along and see where this goes.

He starts driving, and it's easy to tell that he's trying to throw me off. Why? That's what I'd like to know, but I don't say anything. TJ continues on his driving escapade and makes sure that he goes the absolute longest way around to the docks.

After passing Ms. Alice's bakery for the third time, I can't keep quiet any longer.

"TJ, what are you doing? Where are we going? Better yet, what are you up to?"

"Nothing, Dad. I just like to drive," TJ said as a big smile forms on his face. "Just sit back and enjoy the ride. Everything will be clear soon."

I look over at him, and he has a great smile on his face. What a wonderful sight to see. It's the kind of smile you remember from when kids are little. The ones where it makes you feel good to know they love being with you at that moment. I finally give up and decide to be quiet.

Twenty minutes later, we pull into the parking lot for another set of docks from where my boat stays. At first, I think TJ has made a mistake, and just as I'm about to say something, I see *Old Number 7* painted on the back of a boat at the end of the dock. Then I see Bob Wilson give us a waive.

"Okay, TJ, give it up. What's going on?"

"Well, Dad. It's your birthday next month and since we'll only be here two more weeks, I thought I'd get us a day on Bob's boat," TJ said. "Since last time, you didn't get to fish from *The Big One*, or much at all. So—Happy Birthday."

TJ jumps out of the truck and goes around to the back to start unloading the supplies. I'm paralyzed for a moment, nearly breaking down, not because of some missed opportunity to connect with my son like usual, but because I'm overwhelmed by the gift. This gift is one of the greatest in my life, not because it involves fishing or my birthday, but because it involves him and comes from his heart.

Of course, my mind immediately shifts to finances as I open the door and step out of the truck. I remember that it cost around one hundred fifty dollars for the day I took TJ out earlier in the spring, and I know he doesn't have that kind of money.

"TJ, how did you pay for this?"

"Dad, don't worry about it," TJ answered. "It's all good."

How can I not worry? Where did he get the money to do this? Did he borrow it from a friend? Did he work somewhere I didn't know about? Did he call Jen?

"TJ..."

"Dad, don't worry, it's all good. Bob and I have worked it out," he said. "Just enjoy yourself today. I really want you to."

TJ's words are comforting, and as he speaks, I realize that I'm again trying to control everything, and in doing so, I'm sapping the joy out of the gesture. Time to surrender to it and enjoy myself.

Then, it hits me. I know where the money came from. TJ used the money he won from the fishing tournament to pay for it. That's why Bob came up to me at the fish fry and said what he did. My eyes water at the thought, and I quickly make my way to the restroom for a moment of privacy.

I feel a strange feeling that I haven't experienced before—tears of joy. I know that TJ and I might never share another day like this again; yet, for me, I know that no matter what happens from today on, we both will have this day to remember and cherish forever.

As I walk out, TJ is at the boat loading the supplies.

"Come on, it's time to go," he said in his best imitation of me.

"Getting there," I said in my best sarcastic version of him.

Once on the boat, TJ goes off to the front with Luke and Joe. They'd become good friends over the summer and spent a lot of time together around town. Bob asks me over for a cup of coffee and to sit next to him while he guides us out of the dock and toward our first spot. The air is cool for an August morning, and the lake is magnificent in every way.

"I'm monitoring a small pocket of showers in the Northwest. I don't think it'll hit the area until later this evening or tomorrow. But if it does hit tonight, we should be well home by then," Bob said with a calm voice. "Besides, the fishing is good the day before it rains."

"Good. Maybe we'll get lucky."

"I hope so. From what TJ says, you're going to be doing most of your fishing from *The Big One*."

"That's what he told me."

"Did you get to fish from it last time?"

"Nah, just TJ."

"Tom, it's a great experience. There's nothing like being completely focused and using all your muscles to catch big fish. I think you're going to like it a lot."

"Well, I'm looking forward to it. Hopefully, I won't embarrass myself too much."

"Please. I've seen what you bring to the fish fries," he said. "Humility isn't your best quality."

"Well, I'm working on it, so maybe there's hope for me after all."

We ride in the boat for more than an hour to get to the first spot of the day to fish. As I've gotten to know Bob over the course of the summer, I find him to be both interesting and quiet. He's interesting because of the choices he's made in his life—choices that most noticeably cost him money, yet satisfy his need for a quiet, laid-back lifestyle. Since we're both quiet people by nature, conversation has been limited somewhat to encounters of questions and answers. I have the feeling that if I were to open up a little to Bob, then we would probably become great friends. I sense that he thinks about things at a much deeper level than all the surface stuff I usually get from others. The only issue is that we're leaving soon, and my chances of getting to know him better are decreasing by the minute. I should've gotten to know him better before now. Another lesson learned, I guess.

The plan is for us to stop at two prime fishing spots—one in the morning; and the other, after lunch. We've carved out about three hours at each spot to fish before we head back to shore. Since I'm the apparent guest of honor, I get to fish the entire day from *The Big One*.

As we reach the first destination point, Bob turns to me and asks, "Are you ready?"

"Sure."

"Dad," TJ said, as he makes his way from the front of the boat. "Get ready for an adventure you won't forget."

"Hey, I'm ready. Show me the way."

Getting strapped into the chair, I begin to realize what Bob was talking about earlier. The chair feels like a cockpit on a fighter jet or something; especially with all the harnesses, seatbelts and the way the chair swivels back and forth. After lockdown, I'm ready to wreak havoc on the fishing world once again.

As I start to fish, strapped into every gadget conceived by man and looking ever so ready to catch a blue whale, I can't help but think to myself what a wonderful thing TJ has done for me. I quickly glance over to him, and he's looking away. As most parents do when their kids aren't looking, I watch him sitting at the front of the boat and see the wind in his hair. I can't tell you how soothing a feeling it is to watch my boy and know that he's mine. My heart is bursting with joy as I sit here in this moment.

TJ turns and looks around the boat. He catches my eyes on him. Instead of giving me the usual look-off or disgusted frown, which had been so common these last few years, he surprises me with a big, warm smile. It's a smile that says *You're my dad, and I want you to enjoy yourself today.* I smile back, and for that moment, we connect again and ease the tensions of a lot of years.

I learn from Bob that our goal is to find and catch either a rock bass or channel catfish, the largest fish in the lake. I think Bob wants me to catch a trophy fish, so that I'll have something to remember this trip by and to truly enjoy the experience of *The Big One*. The irony, of course, is that no matter if I catch the largest fish ever in the lake or not, I'll never forget this day as long as I live.

I fish the first spot for the full three hours. I'm really beginning to understand the better qualities of *The Big One*, and I start using them to my full advantage. Although I haven't caught the monster of all fish, I do catch plenty for all to enjoy. I've caught an abundance of walleye, bass, and catfish to keep me company and to keep the boys working.

The morning is fantastic. I'm not a person who generally finds joy in very many things, but I'm having a great time. Bob was right all along. The experience does far outweigh the results. I also think that by surrendering to the day and enjoying it for what it is, I'm able to truly take a moment to live and to share that with TJ.

Lunch is delicious as well because Bob brings out a grill, sautés the fresh fish filets from the morning catch, and creates a lunch that most restaurants would kill to serve as its main course. I'm impressed, and I'm not kidding when I tell him he should open a place on the lake.

"No, don't think I could do that again," Bob said with a light-hearted grin. "Been there, done that."

"You've owned a restaurant on the lake before? Not to pry, but how did it go?"

"Tom, it was good. People would come from miles around to dine with us every night. I'd say we were the most popular and most successful place this part of the lake had ever seen."

"Wow! What happened? If you don't mind my asking?"

"It's just like anything else in life, you know. We were successful and made some great money, but ultimately, I didn't wake up everyday fulfilled. I went to work everyday wanting to do something different, and everyday, I became indifferent. It's no way to live."

Yep, Bob and I could be great friends. What an amazing story. What an amazing way to live your life. I'm so envious.

After lunch, Bob takes us to the other fishing spot, a couple of miles farther out, so we can fish the afternoon. He feels that this will give us the best opportunity to find a large channel catfish. I'm already having such a wonderful time that I'd be content to head back and call it a day, but TJ insists that we stay for the afternoon. I think he wants me to make a trophy catch too, so I just go along and keep having a great time.

The results are varied, as I'm able to find a school of walleye and catch quite a few. But, I still have no luck catching the monsters waiting for me below. Eerily, the sky becomes a solid white-gray color, essentially showing no emotion. I've always been a little worried when the sky gets this way because it usually means the unexpected is lurking in the shadows.

I look back at Bob, and he's moved from his post on top of the boat into his captain's chair. He looks at me quickly, and then turns away to watch his monitor more closely. As with any good fisherman, he has his weather monitor going at all times.

"Everything okay?"

"Yeah, I think so. It's strange because the monitor doesn't show any bad weather in the area, but the sky says something different."

"Let me know if you need any help or want us to do anything."

"It should be fine. I'll keep you posted."

I turn back to look at the sky and reel in my fishing line. A solid, white-gray sky is tricky because it can mean a storm is coming, or it can just mean the day is getting hotter than usual. Either way, I don't like it.

Suddenly, a bolt of lightning slashes through the sky like God himself throws it down in a rage. The clouds begin to swirl and darkness slowly, but effectively, covers the heavens. The rains come, and come in a hurry. I've never before experienced a scene change so quickly, and I'm scared.

I look back at Bob, who comes to the door of the captain's room and yells, "Get your life jackets on now! Luke and Joe, get up to the front of the boat and pull anchor. We've got to get out of here!"

TJ is resting on a seat near the entrance to the captain's room when he hears Bob yell. He springs up and goes to get two life jackets—one for him, and the other for me. Actually, Bob had said that if we did get caught in a storm, the safest place on the boat was most likely in the chair. Unless, he had added with his dry wit, the boat flipped over.

As the clouds swirl and the heavens continue opening up, the rain begins to fall harder and the lightning begins to strike more quickly. The rains pour on us like we're nails being pounded by a hammer. The boat begins to rock more wildly as the wind picks up speed. TJ tries to bring the life jacket to me, but as he's walking toward me, he slips on the wet deck and goes down hard.

"Put your life jacket on, now! I'll be fine!"

We hear a blood-curling scream from the front of the boat. I see the scene through the rain and can make out what appears to be Luke lying on the front deck grabbing for his foot. Bob stops the motor and takes off to see if he's okay.

I try to unstrap myself from the chair, but it's difficult to remember where all the straps, latches and belts are locked. As the rain comes down and the boat continues to rock, hail begins to fall. Given my task of trying to get free, it's extremely hard to shield myself from the hail strikes. Each one, it feels, hits me a little harder than the last.

The waves begin to swell higher and higher as the moments pass, and the wind picks up more speed. After getting smacked pretty hard by the hail, I try to hide my face and look down for a moment. When I look back, I see TJ slowly making his way toward me. He hasn't finished putting on his life jacket yet, but he knows I'm defenseless against the elements.

A large wave slaps the starboard side of the boat, and TJ loses his balance. He picks himself up and makes his way back to his feet. As soon as he turns his head in my direction, a hail drop the size of a baseball hits him square in the jaw, causing him to stumble and fall. Since he's on the low end of the boat as the wave slaps it again, his chest lands on the side rail as it swings up to correct itself after dipping under the wave. I watch in horror as he falls over the side of the boat when it dips back under the returning wave. He only has one arm through his life jacket, and I don't know if he's conscious or not.

"NOOOOOOO!"

Got to get out of this thing! Got to get free!

"HELP!"

Oh my God! Got to get these belts off! God help me! Please, God, help me get these belts off! I can't get them off! I can't get them off!

After what feels like an eternity, I'm finally able to unlock the belts and latches, but the final harness won't budge.

Where is it? Where is it?

Fumbling around and pulling at the harness with all my might, I remember I still have my knife. I wiggle my hand into my pocket, get it out, and open it up.

I'm coming TJ! I'm coming!

"TJ!—TJ!" I yell with everything I have.

I cut the last harness, free myself, and hit the deck hard as I make it to the edge of the side rail.

"TJ!—TJ!"

In the water, I see the life jacket about twenty feet away and TJ's partially on top of it. He isn't moving, and every fear of life passes through my body. I see him start to slip underwater as another wave passes over him and my heart sinks.

I look around for something—anything—to help.

Oh God!

Oh God!

I grab the rope used to tie the boat to the dock, put my arm through the loop, and dive in. I swim as hard as I can, trying to not lose sight of the life jacket. About five feet from TJ, I see his arm slip out from the jacket and his body sink in the water.

Oh God—NO!

I dive underwater and swim with everything I have to try and save him. I reach for him, but get nothing. As my body starts to rise to the surface, I force myself to go lower. I reach out again and grab for anything I can get—nothing.

With my chest pounding and begging for air, I push myself deeper, close my eyes, extend my arms and grab one last time for my boy. I feel TJ's shirt on my hand, and I lock my grip as tight as I can and pull with all my might.

I kick my legs hard as I try to pull us both up. I make it high enough to get my head out of the water for a second or two of air. Then I use my strength to pull TJ into a position where his head and body are face up in the water. His weight pushes my head down, and I come up for air every few seconds, but I'm not about to let him go.

My muscles are tired from the strain of keeping us both afloat, and I haven't been able to take a big breath yet. Exhausted, I don't have much more left. Can't give up. Can't give up. I still have the rope around one arm, so I give it one last tug before my body gives out. As we both begin to sink, my life begins to play out in front of me like a bad movie. Is this it? Am I to die with the greatest joy I've ever known in my arms dying with me? What kind of fair is that? I might deserve it, but not him—not my baby; not my baby.

To my surprise, we start moving back against the waves and out of the water like we're being towed. I turn my tired head and see Bob and Joe pulling us in faster than I thought humanly possible. Bob reaches down and grabs TJ out of my arms and hands him to Joe. Then, he turns back and pulls me out of the water just as fast.

Lying on the deck, I can barely move, but I know I have to get to TJ. Bob and Joe immediately start CPR on TJ because he's stopped breathing. Willing myself up, I crawl over to him and grab his arm and lay my head next to his ear.

"TJ, please wake up. I need you to wake up."

Joe grabs TJ's head and breathes two quick breaths into his mouth, and Bob starts the chest pumps again. I begin to sob harder than ever before, as I look at Bob and Joe working with everything they have to save my son.

"TJ, you have to come back. You're everything to me. I can't lose you now because I've just found you again. Please come back to me and let me make it all up to you. I need you son." I quickly search my brain for anything to say. I'm afraid it's too late and the fear of losing him is unbearable. Knowing it might be the last thing I ever say to him, I whisper quietly in his ear, "TJ, Daddy loves you whole bunches."

I close my eyes and sob uncontrollably because I know he's gone forever. The empty, hollow feeling in my body is my soul being ripped apart and voided of existence. There's nothing left, and I'm ready to die. I can't go on without him. I can't live with myself if he's gone. Take me now, God. Please, take me now.

Then, as a dying man's last wish is granted, TJ coughs and begins to spew water out of his mouth. Bob and Joe roll him on his side and he coughs some more. The water keeps coming. A few seconds later, TJ is gasping for air. Finally, the coughing slows and he breathes more easily.

I rise up to a sitting position, grab TJ's head, and hold it close to my body. I don't want to ever let go again, and I cradle his head like I did when he was a baby. During the ride back, I wait every second to be sure that he breathes before I do. I know this is the only thing I can do to remain calm. I thank God with all my soul for saving my baby, and I forevermore become a humbled man.

19 THE NEXT FEW DAYS WERE QUIET AND REFLECTIVE for both TJ and me. TJ spoke rarely after we returned to shore from that fateful outing, and I let him take all the time he needed.

Since we were planning to leave in several days, Jen decided, after much convincing from me, that she would stay home and wait for us to return. As with any mother, her first instinct was to drop everything and run to be with her child, but I told her that TJ was fine and that he needed time to process everything. I know he would've loved to have his mother come and take care of him, but he told me distinctly that he just wanted to be alone for awhile, and he made me promise to keep Jen from coming to see him. Given all that he's been through, I can't go against his wishes on this or anything else right now.

Those first few days back, neither of us was in the mood to fish, so each day I went back to my favorite seat on the porch and just thanked my lucky stars that TJ was still with me. To my delight and surprise, TJ would come out and sit with me for long periods of time. We barely talked, but the communication between us was there and stronger than it ever had been.

Each afternoon, TJ takes a long walk, and when he returns, his mood seems more and more calm, almost spiritual. I don't know what it is, but he seems to benefit from the experience, and that's all I really need to know about it. Usually, when he returns from his walks, there's another basket of food waiting for him at the cabin. Home-cooked meals, fruits and sweets are a regular at our door these days, and TJ is extremely grateful for all the well wishes from the good people of the town. Their kindness has also helped me to realize that in a society where everything is 'super-sized' and in a hurry, there are people who actually stop to think about life and others first. It's refreshing to know that the virtues, we all long to keep, still exist right here in this town and with these good people.

Personally, I've come to love these people, and they all have a special place in my heart. They've accepted us as part of their community and as part of their family. I know that if there is any way that I can, I will try to get back here as much as possible because I want Jen to meet these people and get to know them like I do.

I'm sad that our time here is coming to an end. It's funny, in a sad way, when I think back to when Jen was putting her foot down and sending TJ with me. It's funny, because of how I acted about the whole episode, and it's sad because I felt TJ would ruin my trip and bring me nothing but grief.

What a fool I am! How can anyone—a mother, father, son or daughter—think that spending time with your family is a bad thing? It's only as bad or as good as we make it. Believe me, you come this close to losing someone special, your perspective changes in a hurry and your pettiness goes away.

As I sit in my chair on Thursday evening, two days before we're to leave for home, TJ comes in from his afternoon walk. He makes his way to the porch and sits down beside me. I can see that he has a pleasantness about him, which is something I don't think I've ever seen in him. It isn't only a peaceful, harmonious glow that he carries; it's also a redemptive, mature calm as if death's door has left him in a spiritual place of knowing and understanding.

"Dad," said TJ.

"Yeah."

"I want us to go fishing tomorrow."

"What? Are you serious? Really?"

"Yeah, I'm serious," he said. "I think it's time that we get back out there. Fishing is something I love, and I don't plan to stop now."

"Okay. I guess that's good enough for me. As long as you're sure, then I'm good."

"Great! Let's come back early and then head to one last fish fry. I want to see everyone and thank them before we leave."

The early morning sun broke through the clouds as we headed to Fred's store. I'm still tired from the night before because I couldn't sleep. My mind keeps drifting back to our last outing on Bob's boat, and I have to tell myself to be strong and just let the day happen. Hopefully, that's what I'll do. If not for me, then at least for him.

Honestly, I'm scared to death at what can happen. I think TJ is probably further along than I am at this point. I guess it's just like anything else. You've got to get back up on the horse when you get thrown off. It's a great saying that people say to you when you're down, and sure it's encouraging, but what they don't tell you is that it's a big ass horse to get back on. Nothing is ever easy because if it were, then we wouldn't have such clever idioms to throw around at each other.

Fortunately for us, today is scheduled to be free and clear from any bad weather. TJ and I do our routine like we have from the beginning, and it feels good—therapeutic—to us both. We laugh, reflect and tell stories about our time together. I think we both realize that even though we've had our differences and tough times, we're still family and love each other very much. I also think that when we return to our lives, we'll be different all around, if not better.

We stay on the lake until around two o'clock, catching yellow perch. TJ wants to fish for perch since that's what had ultimately brought us to the lake in the first place. Although the day is hot and muggy, we still manage to catch about ten nice-sized perch—enough to gain us passage into the town fish fry later that evening.

"Dad," said TJ.

"Yes."

"Thanks for going with me today. I just didn't want to leave this wonderful place and have my last time on the lake be negative."

"Honestly, I was worried about it at first, but I'm glad you suggested it."

"Yeah, me too. Today was perfect, and that's what I want to remember."

After resting for a while, TJ comes out on the porch and sits down. We don't speak for several moments, instead choosing to listen to the rhythms of the summer afternoon. There's a certain harmony in nature, like a musical orchestra working closely together to capture the beauty of a classical masterpiece, that we forget to pay attention to sometimes.

"Get some rest?" I asked breaking the silence.

"Yeah, it was nice," TJ answered. "You?"

"A little. This place is relaxing just sitting here."

"Feel like taking a walk with me?"

A walk? I most definitely would like to go on a walk with him. If for no other reason, I'm incredibly curious as to where he goes each afternoon. Besides, I want to go to any place that can make my mood as calm and peaceful as his is when he comes back from his walks everyday.

"Of course, I would."

"Great! Let's go!"

We walk all around town—a pretty good distance from our cabin. It feels good to just relax and have a pleasant walk. From the way people around town greet us, we're reminded that we're home. Our walk takes us by the docks, the boat slip, Fred's store and Ms. Alice's bakery. It's obvious that TJ has been this way many times. He leads me down a dirt road, covered by maple and oak trees, and off the main street. Then, we follow a dirt path through the trees and up a small hill. I don't say anything because it seems clear that TJ wants me to come to this place with him.

As we reach the end of the path at the top of the hill, we enter into a clearing, which overlooks the lake. What a beautiful place it is—so peaceful and calm. I'm impressed with the place, and I have no problem letting TJ know.

"Wow! What an incredible view!"

"It's nice, isn't it?"

"Yes. How did you find it?"

"The other kids from town brought me up here a while ago," he said. "It's supposed to be a secret from the adults, but I think they all know about it and just look the other way."

In the past, I would've gotten upset about hearing how the kids were keeping a secret from their parents, but not anymore. For me, it feels like TJ is letting me into his private world—a place I never thought I would be a part of again. Yet, here he is offering an olive branch to me after all these years. I have truly waited a long time for this, and I'm going to soak up every moment.

"Dad," TJ said, as he sits back against a tree. "I need to ask you something."

"Sure, what is it?"

"I know we've had our differences over the years, and basically, we haven't liked each other too much. But, I have to know something. I have to know why you weren't there for me when I was growing up. I know you were around, but then again, you weren't. It was almost like you shut me out. Did I do something to you to make you not want to be around me?"

I've been trying to better myself in a lot of ways recently. It's strange how the things I've been working on to better myself always creep back into my path when I'm not looking. I guess I knew at some point, I would have to face the music. I think I've worked it out for myself. Obviously, I leave part of the equation unresolved, and sadly, he's the most important part.

"Well, honestly, I don't know how to answer that question, but I'm going to try to do the best I can. I have no excuse for being emotionally cut-off from you as you were growing up. I know it's left you with some emotional scars, and if I could, I'd go back and do it right. But, as you know, I can't do that. All I can do is offer you my word that from now on, I'll always be here for you. I promise you that, Son."

TJ looks around the beautiful scene and doesn't say anything. The truth hurts sometimes, and I can only imagine what he's feeling. I wish I could take it back and get a 'do-over' like we used to when we played football in the backyard. Someone would do something that somebody else didn't like and instead of fighting about it, we would just take a 'do-over' and play it again. It's too bad there are no 'do-overs' in life because I think I'd definitely want to make some things right and learn my lessons a little easier—maybe heal some wounds I've caused.

"I guess I've tried so hard to be my own man and to make my own way that I did things pretty crappy at times. I loved my father a lot, but he was an asshole to me quite often, and I vowed that I wouldn't be that way with you. I vowed that I was going to break the pattern and not be an overly strict, detached father to you. My goal was to be emotionally supportive and loving to you all the time, even when I was disciplining you. I just wanted you to feel loved by your mom and me and have a peaceful security in that.

"Those were my goals, but the reality is that I did the same things to you that my father did to me. It's one thing to love you, which I do, but it's another thing entirely to be loving toward you, which I haven't done. Being loving should be the goal of every parent to his child. It took me a long time and a lot of soul searching here to understand that. As I've said before to you, I'm ashamed of what I have and haven't done. You deserve to know that it's not your fault the way our relationship has turned out through the years. I take the blame because I'm the cause, and I can look you in the eye, man to man, and tell you that. I understand that we may never be close, and if we aren't, then that's a consequence I have brought on myself. But, if you give me the benefit of the doubt and another chance, then I promise you that you can count on me to be the caring, loving father that you want and that you deserve."

"Thank you for saying that to me. I believe you," TJ said. "I have no doubt."

"TJ, one day you'll have children, and you'll understand what I'm telling you and how easy it is to make mistakes and how difficult it is to make it right."

I lean back on the tree right next to where TJ sits. We both look out at the town and the lake. The afternoon is coming to an end and dusk is upon us. The scene is fitting for the conversation we're having.

"Everyday, I take a walk, and I come here to relax and gather my thoughts," TJ said. "I like it because it helps me think."

"I can tell that you like it, and I notice a difference in you when you finish your walks each day. I just wish I knew about this place before now because I could've come up here some too."

"You may have noticed that I leave for my walk everyday at the same time."

"Actually, I did notice."

"Well, I've got my walk timed out so that when I get here and get settled for a few minutes, I get to watch the sunset on the lake," TJ said with a smile. "I think I now understand what you've been talking about all this time when you said it's peaceful and honest."

I shake my head in agreement as he speaks. TJ has grasped one of the most beautiful things I've ever known, and for me, the sentiment is a validation and understanding of my trials growing up and a mirror into my son's life today. Now, TJ is following in my footsteps, out looking for anything tranquil to comfort him. The difference between us both is that he brings me along.

"Ever since the accident, I've been trying to come to grips with everything that happened," he said calmly. "It's funny because you think you're invincible and that nothing will ever happen to you. Then, out of nowhere, your life is almost gone. It's just crazy, but it has made me realize that life is precious, and we shouldn't take it for granted."

"I certainly agree with that. When we came here, I was struggling with a lot of things myself, including your grandfather's death. I've also come to realize that we should make the most of our lives everyday. Life is a funny thing because one minute you can be on top of the world and living large, and the next, you come crashing down and people are kicking dirt in your face."

"Yeah."

"TJ, you're dysfunctional, and I say that with all sincerity and honesty. You're screwed up, and you will be for the rest of your life. I've done emotional damage to you that can't be repaired. So has your mother, and others in your life."

TJ looks up and his face shows a serious look of concern. I turn to him and smile—a big, wide smile—and he smiles back knowing everything is okay.

"Don't worry son, we're all screwed up. Every person, every family, and every relationship has an element of dysfunction in it. My parents passed it down to me, and your mom's parents passed it down to her. Just so you wouldn't feel left out, we've taken the liberty to make sure you have your own set of issues to deal with throughout life."

"That's so depressing," TJ said. "Why does it have to be so gloomy? Why does everyone have to deal with this stuff all the time? It doesn't seem fair."

"Son, life's not fair. It never is. You can't fool yourself into thinking it's going to be fair. All you can do is have the power to make the most of your life, help others, and make a difference. You're already a step closer because you've realized that life is precious and that our time here is short. The next step is to embrace your dysfunction, admit that you're flawed, and understand why you're that way. I'll give you a hint, it has a lot to do with me and your mom."

"I pretty much had that part figured out already."

"Hey, I admit it. I'm the biggest cause—without a doubt. It's the perpetual nature of the beast, I guess. Seriously though, I've only recently become aware of my shortcomings, misgivings and the countless other things about myself that drive people crazy, and I'm working on them to make myself better. Fortunately, you're a lot smarter than I am, and your wisdom and understanding at your age amazes me. Take what you learn about life, love, and harmony, and make yourself a great man. That's all I want for you. If you only remember one thing throughout your life that I say to you, then remember this…

"There are no words to truly describe what you mean to me. It has taken me a long time to understand it myself, but now, I know. You're my light at the end of the tunnel; you're the air that I breathe; and you're the hope and promise of a new day. I love you with all my heart and all my soul, and I would die for you—anytime, anyplace."

TJ looks up at me with his big, brown eyes, tears rolling down his cheeks, and I see the look that I haven't seen since he was four years old. It's the look that says to me, "I'm safe; I'm great; and that I'm his Daddy again." Our defenses are all down now, both his and mine, as I look back into his face with tears flowing down mine.

This is where we've arrived. For TJ, fifteen years of ups and downs, emotional scars and a need for change. For me, many years of battling as a boy growing up then a perpetual battle on the other side as an adult—with no resolution. Now, at least, we arrive here together and leave with a new hope.

"Dad," TJ said, as he reaches out and puts his arms around my neck. "I Love You."

Epilogue

Tom heard the voices of family members in distant conversations. He sat motionless gazing at the wall in front of him.

As with most times, when the mind drifts away, the initial shock of coming back to reality caused him to jump in his chair. To the casual observer, it appeared that he had dozed off and caught himself before falling. Fortunately, as Tom looked around, his family said nothing and the suspecting glances quickly subsided. His reality also reminded him of where he was and the heaviness of the situation returned.

He looked around for Tommy and spotted him looking depressed and upset next to Sara. Tom waived his hand and got Tommy's attention, then motioned for him to come and stand beside him. At first, he looked away and pretended not to be interested, but Tom was persistent. Finally, Tommy gave in, walked over, and stood by his father's side.

"I know you were talking to me a moment ago, and I'm sorry I didn't answer you. What was your question?" Tom asked.

Reluctantly, Tommy answered. "I was supposed to go fishing alone with Grandpa this summer for the first time. He was going to teach me how to fish for perch. Who's going to teach me now?"

With a renewed confidence he hadn't felt in days, Tom answered his son, "I'll teach you, buddy. I'll teach you."

Now, I can go and rest in peace because I know everything will be just fine. I love you, Tom. You've grown up to be a great man.